JAYME & JAYDA

Mother and Daughter with a Special Talent

Order this book online at www.trafford.com
or email orders@trafford.com

Most Trafford titles are also available at major online book retailers.

Note for Librarians: A cataloguing record for this book is available from Library
and Archives Canada at www.collectionscanada.ca/amicus/index-e.html

Printed in Victoria, BC, Canada.

ISBN: 978-1-4269-1514-7 (sc)

*Our mission is to efficiently provide the world's finest, most comprehensive book publishing
service, enabling every author to experience success. To find out how to publish your book, your
way, and have it available worldwide, visit us online at www.trafford.com*

Trafford rev. 9/29/2009

Trafford
PUBLISHING® www.trafford.com

North America & international
toll-free: 1 888 232 4444 (USA & Canada)
phone: 250 383 6864 ♦ fax: 812 355 4082

Dedication

To our daughter Susan for her patient, persistent,
knowledgeable training of the author in the ways of
acceptable grammar which he gladly omitted during days of
"studying literature not grammar."

Acknowlegements

Assistance with this "stubborn"laptop by my care-givers and daughter Susan was critical to the completion of this manuscript. Lessons in grammar from Susan and her proofing of final copy of the manuscript gave respect to this story of my grand daughter and my great granddaughter and their wonderful gifts of helping children find their way in a complex society.

PREFACE

Jayme and Jayda, mother and daughter, are real. The use of horses to help children find their way in this complex world is a proven procedure. It works. The stories of these two ladies from childhood to marriage could be real. Records in the barrel races are a little low, but possible. The rest is fiction from the author's imagination and knowledge from research.

Communication between a rider and horse was demonstrated by a real event in a grand daughter's teenage years. Her father came into possession of an untrained Arabian horse. He had little success training the horse. It was mean and had a mind of it own. Jayme took the challenge and a few days latter when her father came home the "unruly" horse was grazing in the pasture and stretched on its back, sunning herself was Jayme. No bridle, no saddle. Just a short rope that wasn't tied to anything.

Find the reasons behind this talent as we develop wonderful stories of Jayme and later Jayda and their unique abilities to communicate with their filly.

PART I

Jayme

*I Set a World Record and
meet a Soul mate*

"Look out! A little girl has run into the path of the racers!"

"And Jayme Kent is ready to start her run with Star! I understand she hopes to set a new record for the race! She's starting! And the little girl is directly in Star's path!"

"Star has stopped!"

Jayme slide off Star and ran to see the little girl who she recognized as Joyce, whom she and Star had worked with the previous week. Taking her hand they walked towards Star. Looking for a treat, Star nuzzled Joyce. Jayme gave her a treat and Star eagerly took it from Joyce's hand.

"You should not get in the path where the horses run, Joyce. Some of the horses wont recognize you as Star did and you could get hurt.

"I wont do it again, Jayme. I just wanted to greet Star. She wouldn't hurt me, would she? Can I get up on her back?"

"Sure you can. Let me get up first, then Judge Russell will give you a boost?"

By now every body was crowding around to be sure the "little girl"wasn't hurt. Joyce and I turned Star back to the starting place where her mother took Joyce from Star's back.

"Thank you, Jayme. How did you stop Star so quickly?"

"I didn't stop her. She had already stopped when I saw Joyce. I think she recognized an old friend and wanted to see if she had a treat, Bye Joyce."

Needless to say, this race had been thoroughly disrupted. All the officials and concerned adults were huddling to see what should be done.

After a few minutes, I said,

"Star and I are ready. Let's get this race over."

Judge Russell agreed, "time keeper are you ready?"

"Yes, sir, I'm ready."

Star and I had a brief conference, I talked and she listened, and we took off like winners. Star was at her best. She made quick, fast turns not touching a barrel and when we headed home, she practically flew. I had to grab the saddle to keep from falling backwards. Cheers roared at the finish line as it was obvious that it was a record run!

From the time keeper:"my equipment worked perfectly. Time: 14 seconds, flat. A new record!"

Congratulations all around! Especially

from Dad and Mother. I hugged Star and took her outside to cool off. Dad's event was later in the day.

From the public address system: "We have witnessed a great horse, a superb rider, and the unique relationship between a horse and its rider. Judge Russell will hold a press conference in the press room in thirty minutes to answer questions and interview Jayme, her family, and tell of a program of developing this unique relationship between animals and people. I don't think there is room in the press room for Star, but there should be a place just outside."

The press conference gave us an opportunity to emphasize the value of an animal in helping children adjust to the emotions of life. Joyce's mother pointed out that Joyce had not been able to accept the loss of her father, but after an hour with Jayme and Star she became a girl who accepted what life had handed her, and became a normal six year old.

Joyce added, "When Jayme showed me that big ol' Star liked me, and I could ride on her I believed my Daddy would have liked Star. She's my friend."

Judge Russell made an important point reminding everyone that Jayme's conduct was critical to the success of the relationship.

"Notice that she did not scold Joyce but met her where she was emotionally, and proceeded to use her earlier association with Star to continue the healing that had already begun. Agreeing to let her ride Star, kept the confidence she had learned. Joyce will not run out in the race track again. But the memory of being greeted by a friend —Star —as she nuzzled her pocket for a treat, and to ride with Jayme again, will be in her memory bank for many years."

Participating in a real barrel race was new and exciting for me. Our family had driven to San Antonio to the Annual Stock Show, and Rodeo pulling our horse trailer with my two year-old filly, Star and Dad's horse, Patch. I was looking forward to my first barrel race competition. It turned out to be more exciting than I had anticipated.

Calf roping-tie-down was a very popular event, so it was

scheduled just before the evening performance in the arena. This event begins with a small calf penned in one of the pens along the side of the arena. On the right side of the gate to the pen the contestant positions his horse facing away from the gate. He will have two ropes in case he misses with the first one, plus a small rope usually held in his teeth to tie the calf's legs together. On the left side of the gate, his assistant will position his horse also facing way from the gate. A barrier – usually a rope is strung across in front of the horses to prevent a premature start. When both riders signal they are ready, the calf is turned loose to run and the barrier in front of the horses is released.

The contestant, throws a rope on the calf, jumps off his horse, grabs the line which now has one end holding the calf and the other end tied to the saddle on his horse (which is trained to keep the line tight) he throws the calf down and ties three legs of the calf together and throws his hands in the air to indicate he is finished. If the calf gets up by itself within ten seconds, the rider does not score.

What's the other rider doing? His job is to break with the other rider and keep the calf running straight away from the rider who hopes to lassos the calf. Timing is critical. More than ten seconds often keeps the rider out of the money.

Announcing the next contestant in the calf roping tie down event, the public address announcer said: "Number four is George Kent and his 12 year-old, daughter Jayme. Jayme, rodeo officials just received conformation that your barrel run was a world record. Congratulations! (Star and I knew it was.)"

There were three heats in the calf roping event, and Star, Patch, Dad, and I won all three and first place in the event. It was a joyful ride home. We congratulated ourselves, sang songs and found the road home much shorter than the one going to San Antonio.

We didn't know at the time, but that would be my only time to ride in the barrel race. Star was beginning to limp slightly, and our vet examined her carefully a month after our ride in the rodeo.

When he had completed his exam, he came in the house for a cup of coffee.

"Is Jayme home? I think she should hear this report."

"I think she is just coming in. Is it that bad?"

"Yes and no, I would like to tell her what I found."

When I walked in the kitchen, Dr. Smith greeted me with,

"Hi Jayme. You got here just in time for us to talk about Star."

"I am always ready to talk about Star. She's a real hero, you know."

"That's what I hear all over the country. She is a fine horse. I am a little concerned about the slight swelling in her right front leg. Would you like to go and let me show you what I found?"

"Yes."

The result of this examination and later checks caused us to decide, 'no more barrel racing, no more rodeo,' but I can still ride her for many years and we can make turns and gallop, but no quick turns to put pressure on her right front leg.

I wanted to cry and did. But my life was so full--- basketball, band and moving on to high school. Star and I had had a wonderful and fulfilling experience with Dad and we would continue to have good times together.

Parties (and boys) were becoming more and more a part

of my life. Graduation parties from the eighth grade were being planned by several groups of students, but some didn't share my idea of a good time. Mother always wanted me to enjoy life, so she asked if I would like to invite a group to our house to celebrate the end of middle school

"Would I? Yes! Could I start on the invitation 'list' now?"

In a few minutes, I had a list of friends that would exceed the capacity of our house to entertain.

"Mother, I have thirty names on my list and I'm not through. How many guests can we have?"

"Let's think about it. We can seat 20 around our dining room table, and we might squeeze five more by setting up the card table. Also, we only have dishes enough for twenty."

Little brothers are usually just a nuisance as far as parties are concerned, but at that moment my brother Ken came up with a brilliant idea.

"Why don't you set up a buffet table, give each guest a tray and let them help themselves. You could us plastic plates and utensils that way you could have as many as can move around in the house. Eating is secondary to the party. Being girls, they will want to chatter with each other. Dad and I will set up a table for the buffet in the kitchen and make sure there are extra trash cans. We can fill the wash tub with ice, and you can put a variety of drinks there and ice tea on the kitchen cabinet. I think you should make plans for some group activities for your guests as they share their ideas about high school and maybe College. I think we have some videos of school activities."

"When did you learn how to plan parties, Ken? I think those are great ideas, don't you Mother?"

"Yes, that will solve many problems. Thank you, Ken. Let's look at dates."

"Most of the groups are planning on the weekend after classes end. It will mean some will already have left on vacations. A few of those on my list may have to take some finals, so I would like that to be behind them. How about Tuesday, May 26?"

"There are boys on my list, Ken. So you are invited even though you won't graduate until next year. You can plan your party then."

"Thanks, I assumed I would 'be around.' You will need my help. Do you want to get on the computer and design an invitation to announce the greatest party ever held?"

Everyone invited came or sent regrets. Several parents thanked Mother and Dad for hosting the party, and several came to assist with the fun. It was a wonderful party! Ken was right. Food was secondary but essential. We had a few guidelines to stir conversation. Everyone wanted to share their plans for high school electives. Several, like me were continuing with basketball. Most of the members of the band were continuing with that elective.

"What about college?" asked Ken.

"One thing at a time," replied one of the girls.

A few started talking about their favorite universities, but high school was really on their minds.

"Are you going to compete in any rodeos, Jayme?" asked one of the boys who was also interested in riding.

"No, Star needs more time to heal her right front leg. I find time to ride most days. She is still a very wonderful horse and it is fun to ride her even if we can't make the fast turns that we did in the barrel race."

"Has anyone broken your record on the barrel race?"

"No, not even close. As you know from riding her, she is a special horse. When we turned for the final sprint, I whispered in her ear, 'go Star.' I thought I would slip out of the saddle she took off so fast."

"You think she knew what you said?"

From the boy who also rides, "She may not have known what the words were, but she got the message. Animals sense our feelings, and when we have become their friend they will respond."

I found a moment later when I could thank my friend for his support. Conversation returned to high school, college and plans for the summer. At the agreed time for the party to end (1:00A.M.) Dad and the other parents announced it was time to call parents if rides were needed. Ken, I and our parents were deluged with thanks for a great party. One they all enjoyed.

My summer was filled with shopping for clothes, going to swimming parties, a few birthday parties and mentally getting ready for the next step in my "growing up."At our first meeting with teachers including the band director, I was impressed with the importance of high school. Our grades would now become a part of our official scholastic record. Being accepted by our favorite university would depend in part on that record. Also, it would be a factor in awarding scholarships. We had heard all of this before, but it took on greater significance as it became a part of our scholastic record for college and beyond. Most of us just enjoyed the challenge and being together. Boys became more important as they were a part of classwork and an active social life. Those of us who had a church background found that it was not only increasingly guiding us in making decisions, scholastically, but also in the choice of friends and activities.

A quick review of my wardrobe was shocking. I had grown three inches and put on five pounds since the previous season. Also, styles had changed. So off to the mall. This was not much help. Styles had really changed. Skirts were well above the knees. Shorts were really short, nothing suitable for school. We met my classmate Alice and her mother running into the same problem. Going to the food plaza for a break we found Betty, another classmate and her mother raising the same questions about clothes.

Suddenly, I had an idea.

"Alice and Betty, we could put our heads together and write our own 'dress code.' I think there are some other girls who share our ideas about school dressing."

"I'd like to do that," agreed Betty and I know June and Eileen have tastes similar to ours."

"Let's put some ideas on this napkin," suggested Alice.

In a few minutes, we had some guidelines for our new wardrobes. We decided they should be called guidelines to avoid the impression they were mandatory or maybe a "dress code" from the school administration.

Mother raised an interesting question,

"Where are we going to find clothes that fit your guide lines?"

No one had an answer. As if she had heard the question, a member of the store's staff who knew Betty's mother, stopped to see if we were finding what we wanted. We "unloaded" on her—politely. She pulled up a chair and complemented us on what we had done and added,

"I think I can help. If you have a few minutes, let me show you a part of our store that you may have overlooked."

In an hour, the three of us and our mothers had our new wardrobes well in hand with clothes we liked. We thanked

Shannon, our new found assistant, and asked if we could tell other girls to ask for her when they come to shop. She, of course, would love to help others.

When we checked out at the cashier, we discovered our bills had been reduced twenty percent. How nice!

With this major decision behind us, we concentrated on summer parties and who was going to be in whose classes this fall. Band practice for freshman began almost before we realized summer was nearly over. One of the first things we had to learn in band was how to march and play our instruments at the same time. It wasn't hard for those of us in the percussion section, but it was critical that we learn the formations and keep the beat at the right tempo. It was fun. The older players helped us learn to march and play at the same time.

Alice, Jean and I had played basketball together since grade school, so we knew how each other played. We had learned where each would be on the floor in different situations. This made it possible for us to make our passing effective. All three of us took basketball as one of our electives. At the first meeting of the basketball squad the couch surprised everyone when she said;

"I understand that we have three freshmen on our squad who made quite a reputation on the middle school team. Let's find out how good they really are. Jean, Alice and Jayme would you take on three top players from last year's team for a ten minute scrimmage?"

Three from last year's team took the ball at their end of the court and quickly worked the ball down for an easy lay-up, which Alice blocked. Jean grabbed the rebound. I was already down the floor and took Jean's long pass for an easy lay-up.

The next time one of their guards tried for a three-pointer from the top of the key which bounced off the ring, because I was in her face as he shot. Again, Jean got the rebound and Alice and I were both at our basket and added two points. At the end of the ten minutes the score was 14 to 4 in our favor.

"Not bad,"commented the couch. "I assume those of you who will compete for a spot on this year's team took note of some of your competition. Thanks, girls."

This did not guarantee us spots on the team, but it was a good start. We did make the team, and our team went on the win the state championship my senior year.

Junior Prom was the social event of the year at Rutgers High School. Rumors as who was going with who floated across the campus like dust in the air. I accepted an invitation early from a boy I had known since grade school. We had similar ideas about how to have a good time. Ken didn't have to remind us how to handle a crowd at a party. Dad and Mother had already talked with other parents and our "after-prom"party was well in hand. Everyone was welcome, but we needed to know who was coming a week before the prom in order to have ample supplies on hand.

The Prom was scheduled to close at 1:00 A.M. Our house would be available after 1:15. One of the parents was a professional photographer, and said he would be available to take pictures until 2:30. A buffet breakfast would be ready at 4:30. Going home time was 6:30. The schedule was prepared by students and parents.

What a party! Most of our class came to our house and no one wanted to go home. Fatigue (and parents) finally won and by 8: A.M. every one had left, and we thought about cleaning up. Surprise! Five parents came to help, and in thirty minutes our house was back to "normal."

Graduation from high school was filled with ceremonies, parties and visits to universities to learn what courses were offered and if scholarships were available.

My goal was to prepare for law school. One university offered to assure me a place in its law school and pay my tuition and fees through pre-law and three years of law school, if I would play on their basketball squad for two years. That was tempting, and Dad, mother and I spent hours putting pencil to the value of such a deal. It was a good law school and the university had an excellent reputation. When Alice and Jean accepted a scholarship at the same university I decided to go for the deal that offered the scholarship and playing on their basketball team. Alice, Jean and I would have two more years to play together. Sounded like fun!

What was Star doing all this time? I found time to ride her most days and we could trot a little as long as we didn't canter or make quick turns. She seemed to be getting stronger and barely limped. Another plus for the university I chose, was that it was an easy drive to home and I could continue to spend some time with Star. Her leg seemed to have healed and Dr. Smith said I could ride with Dad in the calf roping event, if I wanted to. I wanted to and Dad and I got in a few times to practice.

At the rodeo we were again announced as a father-daughter team. When the barrier was released, Dad, Patch, Star and I broke after the calf. Dad had an almost perfect run, and we went on to win the event. Star seemed to enjoy running again, and her leg didn't bother her any more.

Our church youth choir scheduled a mission trip to New York City in June. I learned that there would be a rodeo in the city at the same time. Our choir would be holding Bible studies for teenagers in several churches in New York City, but we would have one day for sight seeing. My friend Don, who also liked rodeo and horses, teamed up with me and we convinced a sponsor to let us go to the rodeo on our sight-seeing day.

We had just settled in our seats at the rodeo when the barrel race began. The first two contestants made good runs with times below 16 minutes. The third rider tipped over a barrel so was disqualified. The public address announcer:

"I have been informed that the holder of the world record of 14 seconds in the barrel race is in our crowd today. If you are here Jayme Kent, would you stand so we can recognize you?"

Of course, I stood and waved to the crowd which gave me a standing ovation. (I liked being famous.) I also asked Don to stand with me. The rest of the rodeo was interesting, but being recognized in "New York City" was the high light for me. Soon after the announcement about my record, a man approached Don and me. He had a "press" tag on his jacket so we were not concerned. He introduced himself as Pete Wright, a sports reporter with the New York *Times*. This got our attention.

"Rodeos do not have a high priority with the *Times* as you may suspect. But I enjoy them and so I came not expecting a story," commented Pete. "But, Jayme you have made my day. Would you mind visiting with me a few minutes about barrel racing?"

"I would be pleased to talk about barrel racing and my wonderful horse, 'Star.'"

In a few minutes, Pete had information for an interesting story for the *Times*. He promised to send me a copy.

Don and I watched some more rodeo but our day of "sightseeing"was about over, and we returned to the choir and prepared for the trip home. Don bragged about being with a "famous"person and told everyone how I was recognized in New York City. It was a wonderful trip, but the high light for me was to be noticed in New York City.

Back home our family suddenly realized that college was just around the corner. Freshmen orientation was in three weeks. I needed to see where I would be living, what furniture I could have, would I have a room mate, and what clothes I would need.

Jean, Alice and their parents were at orientation and we swapped ideas and information

The president of the university welcomed us as the new freshmen class. I thought his comments were timely and worth remembering. He stressed the fact that we were now "on our own."

"Your teachers will be willing and anxious to help you do your best, but they will not wake you up in the morning, or check to see if you have prepared your lessons. Parents, be ready to accept phone calls and listen to all conversations commenting when appropriate. Above all, assure the students of your love and support. The first semester in college is quite a change in routine and pressure. But it can be very rewarding. One of our psychology professors offered this advice to new students, "Be friendly to all, but choose your close friends carefully."

"Welcome, I hope to see each of you at graduation."

While Jean, Alice and I were checking out our rooms in

the athletic dorm a girl introduce herself and welcomed us to the university.

"My name is Pat and I will be on the basketball squad. In fact, I have been honored to be named captain this year. I usually am assigned as "point guard"but sometimes I play center. Your ability to play a great passing game has become well known in our squad. That's great. We need you and we plan to go to state this year."

"Thank you, Pat. In case you have not heard our names, I'm Jayme, this is Alice and this is Jean. Excuse me, each of us have our parents with us for orientation. (Our parents introduced themselves.) Will we have a team meeting this fall?"

"I have not heard, but I expect Coach Betty will want to start as soon as registration is complete. She is not one to waste time, and she will be especially anxious to meet the new members of the squad. We probably will have some 'walk-ons,' and she will want to meet them. She knows about you, but don't be surprised if she gives you a chance to see what you can do."

"She seems like a nice person,"commented Alice's mother. We all agreed.

Back home and get organized. A visit to our favorite sales lady at the department store was a 'must.' Then to make a list of what to take. My cell phone and laptop were 'must have' items. Good shoes were essential (uniforms were provided)."

Mother and Dad helped me "settle"in my room. Laptop hooked up, picture of Star on the wall, a photo of my family and I was ready to complete registration. Alice, Jean and their parents were doing the same. Coach Betty had posted a notice of a team meeting the next afternoon. She asked that we pick up our uniforms in the morning, and be dressed for playing at the meeting in the afternoon.

Coach Betty had obviously done her home work as she greeted each of us by name. She welcomed us to what was going to be the best team in the history of the school, and urged us to think "State Champions"as that is what we expect to be.

"I expect each player to do your best and capitalize on your special talents. But don't forget that we win or lose as a team,"was Coach Betty's challenge

"Now a quick shoot around."

This was a familiar routine and it was interesting to see the different style of each player.

"Now, for some fun. Members of last year's team put on white shirts. Jean, Alice, Jayme, Joan and Margaret leave on your black shirts. Alice, assume the position of point guard on your team. Pat take your team on the right side basket and bring the ball out to start a short scrimmage."

This was fun. We (black shirts) soon had a six point lead.. Coach Betty whistled us to stop, and gathered the entire squad around her.

"We are going to be good this year. 'State Champion' is well within our reach. I liked the way you black shirts passed. I have heard that Jayme, Alice and Jean have played together since they were strong enough to hold a basketball. It shows. I encourage each of you to learn how they anticipated the moves of team mates. We are a team! We have the floor for another fifteen minutes, if you want to shoot around some more."

Alice, Jean and I spent the time learning names, and talking about our playing experiences and styles. I learned that two other players were planning to go to law school. I liked that. Winning the state championship was not assured, but it would be exciting.

Near the beginning of my sophomore year, we began to think about repeating as state champions. We decided we were that good. Much to my surprise, I was elected as captain of the team for the coming year. Coach Betty switched me to point guard. It was an honor and I told myself to be my very best.

During our practice sessions, I noticed a good looking young man, obviously a member of the boy's basketball squad, sitting in the second row of the bleachers. That didn't surprise me as visitors often came to watch us practice. But this boy came every time. Out of curiosity, I asked one of our players if they knew who our regular visitor was.

"That's Frank Johnson captain of the boys' team,"quickly responded two of our girls.

"He's good looking, isn't he? I am told he's also a nice guy."

A few days later as I was walking from our dressing room to my room, Frank Johnson walked beside me.

"My name is Frank Johnson. May I walk with you? Would you join me for a cappuccino?"

"Yes, I would enjoy that. I understand you play basketball."

"Yes, and I have been watching you play. You have an unusual sense of what the game is all about. Have you played a lot?"

"Since I could hold a ball. Three of us have played together since we were in the first grade. We were state champions in middle school and in high school. So we should know a bit about the game. I was told that you are captain of this year's boys team. Congratulations!"

"And to you, I know you are captain of your team," responded Frank.

"We better win this year to uphold our reputations. Thanks for the cappuccino, Frank. I enjoyed visiting with you. I need to go and get my notes for my biology class."

"I enjoyed it too, Jayme. Let's do it again."

I called Mother to share my experience with Frank. She was pleased and commented that he sounded like someone who would be fun to know. Frank and I did have more cappuccinos and even worked in a movie and supper at the favorite bar-b-que restaurant.

Before the basketball season began I went home for a weekend to visit my family, which included Star. Changing into my riding britches I joined Star in the pasture. She greeted me at the fence and nuzzled my pockets for a treat. Jumping on her back she started walking. After a few yards, she stumbled and fell forward. I slipped off her back and looked see what had happened. The ground was level, but her right front leg was bent at a strange angle.

"Down Star," I urged her, and she slid down on her side and put her head on my lap. Dad had been watching from the barn and came running and talking on his cell phone.

"What happened, Jayme? Did she step in a hole?"

"I could not see any unevenness in the ground. Look at her right front leg. It looks broken!"

"Dr. Smith was on a call just down the road and he will be here soon. In fact, he is driving by the barn now."

"What has happened to our world famous horse?"

"I don't think I am going to like what you are going to tell me, Dr. Smith. Look at her right front leg. The one we worried about a few years ago."

Dr. Smith looked at the leg, and it was obvious that it was

out of normal shape. He felt of the other front leg and also the two back legs. Star did not seem to be in a lot of pain, but lay quietly with her head on my lap. I stroked her head and talked to her.

By now Mother and Ted had joined us. Mother asked me if I was hurt.

"Not physically, Mother. But I think I have lost Star!"

I saw Dr. Smith and Dad whispering, and I was quite sure I knew what they were saying. A horse with a broken leg is virtually impossible to nurse to recovery. They have to be put in a harness, and not put any weight on the leg while it heals —weeks, maybe months. They rarely recover and are miserable during the healing process. My mind had already crossed the line of decision. She must be 'put down' and now before she suffers.

Dad and Dr. Smith came and sat beside me. Doctor Smith told me, her right front leg and ankle were broken, and the other three legs are beginning to show some deterioration. If she were a human, I think the diagnoses would be cancer of the bone. I'm not sure we have a name for it in animals.

"I do not want Star to face any more suffering. Let me have the injection, Doctor."

"Is that what want, Jayme?"asked Dad.

"Yes, she has been a wonderful companion, but nature has intervened and it's time for her to go."

"Here is the syringe. She will not feel anything, and her body will gradually slow down and quit."

"Start it for me, Doctor."

"Sure. We will put it in the large vein in her neck."

As Dr. Smith started the injection, I reach over and put my hand over his, and together we erased any possible pain for Star. In less than a minute, Star's head relaxed and she went wherever great hoses go. I silently thanked God for the wonderful years with Star. Also, I thanked Dr. Smith for his help and for his understanding.

"Be on the lookout for Star #2. She is or will be out there some day."

I told Dad, Mother and Ken I would join them is a few minutes. And Dad, "please call the man to pick up Star's body."

I wanted a few minutes with the memory of Star. As I recovered my emotions, I reminded myself that God has a plan for each of our lives and He loves us. The years I had with Star are an example of that love. I believe He has many more years for me to serve Him, and I look forward to more exciting and fulfilling experiences. Will Frank Johnson be a part of them? God knows, and I will know at the appropriate time.

Joining the family for our evening meal I shared with them my feelings, and my faith that God does love us. To say the years with Star were now in our forgotten past would be untrue and unreal. There will always be that wonderful period in our family's lives when Star was in the forefront. But it will be overshadowed by events yet to come. Ken overwhelmed me when he said, "I'm glad you are my sister!"

Back to basketball and pre-law classes. Back to playing with the team and sharing our skills. It was refreshing and relaxing. We were good and we continued to win. It was a fun experience, and one that I needed. I kept looking for Frank, but he didn't visit the gym. After about a week he called me,

"Can we have dinner at the bar-b-que restaurant tonight?"

"Yes, what time?"

"I'll pick you up at your dorm about 5:30. Is that o.k.?"

"Fine, see you then."

Frank greeted me with a big hug, which I didn't resist. I didn't ask where he had been, but let him tell me what he wanted me to hear. It wasn't long in coming. As we walked to the restaurant, he began.

"I have missed you, Jayme. It seems like a life time since we last talked. How have you been?"

"O.K. but tell me about your absence from the gym for several days."

"My Dad has not been well for many years, and last Friday my brother called and said I should come home. Dad was failing and Mother wanted all of us home for a few days. When I got home it was obvious that Dad was worse. His emphysema had almost stopped him from breathing. We checked him in the hospital, but he didn't improve and on Wednesday he passed away. I think he just became tired of struggling to breath."

"I'm sorry. Losing a parent is a tragic event. Is your mother doing o.k.?"

"Yes, she is. I think all of us knew this would happen. When it does it's still a shock. My brother will be with her, and we have some help each day for a while. My brother is taking care of necessary details including having Dad's will probated. Our family is not rich, but we will survive. I need to be able to help more so I am switching from pre-med to physical therapy which I can complete in a year, and there are plenty of jobs in that field. Your eyes tell me you have had some unhappiness recently. Tell me about it, Jayme."

"What happened to me does not compare with the loss of your father. I did have to put down my companion and friend, Star. Her bones were deteriorating, and her right front leg and ankle were broken. I could not ask her to suffer through treatment of a broken leg. Also, other bones were showing weakness. So we put her down while I held her head in my lap. I thanked the Lord for the years we had had together, and asked Him to guide me in the next phase of my life."

"I'm sorry and thank you for sharing this with me. I know now why your eyes reflect sorrow. It is right that you shed tears. With your permission, let me join you as we together move on with our lives. We have much to be thankful for, and I believe there is much more to come. Basketball needs to be our focus till this season is over and we celebrate at least one state championship. May I offer a suggestion?"

"If it's a happy one, yes."

"It will be for me. Each Sunday let's check our schedules for the coming week, and find one day we can spend time together, a dinner, a movie or just time to talk. I don't mean to limit our time together to one day, but that may be the best we do for now."

"I would like that, Frank. Thank you for suggesting it."

The next weeks were busy but exciting. Our team was even better than last year. We "coasted" through the schedule and were soon looking forward to another state championship. Frank's team was good but they had three crucial games that could knock them out of contention for the state title. We cheered them on, and the last game went to over-time and our boys squeaked by with a last minute free throw by non-other than Captain Frank.

Our plans to have some time together each week worked. Some weeks it was just to have a visit, but, I was finding that I looked forward to our time together more and more. Our ideas and personal goals had few conflicts. I shared my feelings with Mother and Dad almost every day. They were encouraging, and didn't object to making much of our conversation being about 'Frank and me."

Both championship games would be played in the state capitol and on the same day. I encouraged Dad to attend and bring Mother and Ken. Frank had already convinced his brother to attend and bring their mother. Dad had told me that he would like to host a dinner after games for both of our families.

"I'm looking forward to this weekend in addition to our basketball games,"commented Frank as we finished our luscious desert. We will both meet each others parents, and they will get to meet each other and us. We couldn't have planned it better. Maybe the Lord pushed us this way."

"It should be interesting. I specially look forward to meeting your mother. She must be a special person to have reared a young man like you. I know my unbiased brother Ken will not lack for an opinion (which he will share with our family later)."

The last week before the championship games all focus was on preparation of the teams. Our girls team didn't expect any problem. Frank and the boys were concentrating on play of their opponent for the championship. They were confident, but aware they would need to be at their best. Frank and I had only a few minutes during the week to hold hands and say a quick prayer.

To report all the conversation and reactions of this special occasion would take pages and would be unproductive. I will just say we both won our games, and the atmosphere of our meeting with our families was congenial and friendly. Frank's mother was the 'special' lady I had anticipated meeting.

As we each said our goodbyes and prepared to leave for our respective homes I was able to give Frank's hand a squeeze that said, "this was fun and aren't we glad?" We would put our thoughts in words next week at our "regular" meeting --- no! We couldn't wait. As soon as we returned to the campus we found each other and taking hands we interrupted each other saying our reaction to the weekend. We agreed it confirmed our feelings for each other.

During a pause in our conversation Frank asked,

"Will you marry me, Jayme? I love you as I thought it was not possible to love so positively and deeply."

I was not surprised, but excited. "Yes, Frank I love you and will accept your invitation to share life with you! Let's talk about the timing of such a wonderful event. You need to make the transition to physical therapy, and I have three years of law ahead of me. Should we wait until we have some of this behind us?"

"We do have some adjusting in our schedules during the next few years. We could do this as two married sweethearts. Let's enjoin the moment and see what comes next. I sincerely believe the Lord will guide us. In the meantime, can we tell our families?"

"I think so. But let's spend some time together first. There so many things we can share. Are you a late sleeper? Do you like breakfast? Are children part of your dream? Will I be more attractive all dressed up or do you like shorts and peddle pushers?"

"I like you however you are dressed! If the occasion suggests it, I would love to see you dressed like the princess you are. Breakfast is fine if you will share it with me."

"I'm sorry to interrupt this 'love fest,' Jayme. But Coach Betty would like to see you in her office," reported Pat.

"Thank you, Pat. Can you keep a secret for a few days— really keep it?"

"It's no surprise and almost not a secret—you two are getting married. What's the date?"

"How did you know? We just decided a few minutes ago. We haven't even talked about a date."

"It has been quite obvious to us who observe two people together. Congratulations! Are you going to tell Coach Betty?"

"I don't know. Frank, come with me to see Coach Betty."

Coach Betty didn't seem surprised that Frank was with me. "Thank you 'champions,'"she said as she greeted us.

"What I have to say is for Jayme, but if my observation is correct it will be of interest to Frank, also. I don't need to tell you, Jayme, that your contribution to our team these past two years has been every thing we could ask for. It has been fun and two state championships in a row are very rewarding. I am sure you are aware that your obligation to the university was for two years. You do not need to play another minute for this school. I would love to have you for your four years of eligibility, but I'll settle for one year at a time. I have talked with the university president, the dean of the law school and the chairman of the scholarship committee. This is what we can offer. You will play one more year with our basketball program. In return, your academic schedule will be modified to give you the essential material at the end of next summer for your Batchelor's Degree. You would then be eligible to complete your law degree the following three years. Our agreement to waive all fees and tuition through law school still applies. Frank, the lab work for your physical therapy classes can be done with our basketball teams! What do you think?"

"WOW! What a deal!"I exclaimed. "You mean I could play another year with this fantastic team?"

"Yes, and I would like you to continue as point guard, and help me bring the other players to the level of understanding of the game that you show every time we play."

"I glanced at Frank and he nodded a yes."

"Coach Betty we have a confession to make."

"You are getting married."

"How did you know? We just decided a few minutes ago and we haven't talked about a date."

"When you have watched as many students as I have, some things become obvious. The timing often is uncertain but the end result rarely disappoints me. Congratulations Frank! You are a privileged person to have a lady with the beauty and character of Jayme accept your proposal."

"I know and thank you for reminding me."

"I hope this possible change in plans will not keep you from joining us next year."

"Can I have some time to digest all of this? We haven't even told our parents. Frank spoke for both of us as we confirmed our decision, 'God will guide us through whatever comes our way. We truly believe He will. We hope our timing coincides with His."

"I assume that if we get married during the next year, I would not have a room at the athletic dorm."

"That is correct. For obvious reasons, men can't have residence at the girl's athletic dorm. If that becomes a problem, let me see what arraignments can be made at other dorms."

Frank and I found a place to sit and ponder this new information. It was exciting, but was not a quick answer to our question of when –not if—we would get married.

"We better tell our families, Frank. The rest of the world

seems to know we will be married. I think that is nice. But our families need to know of our plans."

"Agreed. Do you have some times in mind?"

"No, I don't. I would like to tell your mother, in person. I think it will be especially meaningful to her. Can we drive there today?"

"Yes, we can if we leave now."

"Let's go and I'll call my family from your house."

Arriving at his house, his mother did not seem upset or even surprised to see us at this unusual time. Taking our hands she asked, "When is the wedding?"

Now I was sure our little 'secret' was as the song says, "Our little secret is a secret no more."

"We have not told my family. Let me get them on the phone."

"Hello, this is Jayme. Dad, if you have not heard, Frank and I are getting married. It seems most people we talk to have already heard or have guessed. We are at Frank's home and just gave the good news to his mother. I'm going to put my phone on the speaker phone so we an all talk, Dad."

"Hey, every one. Jayme is on the speaker phone from Frank's home and they are telling all of us the great news that we have been expecting. They are getting married."

"Wonderful! Frank, it is exciting to know that you will be a part of our family. Have you talked about a date?"

"Yes, we have talked about it, but no decision yet. Mother, we want to come to our house and tell you in person how happy we are. We can be there in about an hour."

"We will be looking for you. Mrs. Johnson, can you come with them? We can celebrate together."

Just then Frank's brother, Bob, came in the door waving a piece of paper at Frank. Frank looked at it and asked,

"What is this all about, Bob?"

"Let's all sit down at the table and I'll bring you up to date. We all knew that Dad was a great guy. His love was real and it was specific. Let me share with you what I mean. This deposit ticket for $100,000 is the proceeds from a life insurance policy naming Mother as beneficiary. His lock box also contained a mortgage cancellation policy payable on his death."

"Is this today's mail? I see a letter from my favorite university. Let's see what it has to say for the good of our country. (Opens the envelope and shouts) "Your request for a scholarship has been approved! It's not raining pennies from heaven, it's raining dollars. By the way, when are you two getting married?"

"Now I knew the rest of the world must know."

Our visit to my family was exciting, and we took off from where we were at the basketball tournament, friendly and like family. Bob had gone with us, and he and his mother returned home thanking their late husband and father for his constant love in making provisions for them after he was gone.

Frank and I drove back to the campus wondering aloud how our lives had moved forward so fast, and what blessings had come to us in less than 24 hours. We agreed this was a confirmation of our love for each other.

The next morning over a cup of cappuccino and toast we silently wondered what next. Frank broke the silence with,

"You must have slept well, you are so beautiful."

"I did once I quit thinking about us. We are so blessed to have discovered each other. And all of our family and our close friends expected it. Let's find a place where we can write down some of the decisions we need to make. We have already made the big one, 'we will get married.' It is not a question of 'if' but 'when.'"

"Here are some facts we should talk about. One, I can have another year of basketball and with two summer sessions I can have my bachelor's degree. Law school can be completed in not more than three years. Two, you can complete your physical education training by this time next year."

"Expenses? My fees and tuition are paid. I think Dad will continue to send me a small allowance. I have a small savings account of my own. So I can be financially o.k. through law school. How does your situation look financially?"

"Now that Mother and Bob will not need the help, I will be o.k. for the next year. Then I should be able to get a regular job with a regular pay check."

"Jayme, suppose we get married next week? Wouldn't all of these conditions hold for the next year? We would need to find housing. But that shouldn't be too difficult."

"Unless I get pregnant the first week. We would welcome the darling little friend, but we would need to do some revised budgeting. Maybe we should talk to our parents -- no, we know what they would say 'wait a year.' We might agree but let's let it be our decision. Enough discussion. I need a hug."

Frank and I were busy the next week getting enrolled for the summer session. I needed to get the courses that would let me complete work for Bachelors degree the following summer. Frank's schedule was arranged so he would get his certification in physical education by the end of the coming school year.

""Coach Betty and I agreed I would spend one hour each day working with our basketball players. We had three "walk-ons" and I wanted to see their level of play."

At the end of the week, Frank and I sat down to see what time we could have together. We agreed to continue our pattern of insisting on having time each week.

"WHOA, that doesn't sound like a schedule for newlyweds. More and more events were making getting married now more difficult. Maybe we should delay the wedding until next year. NEXT YEAR! That seemed like a life time away!"

We had not discussed the kind of wedding we would have. Frank asked,

"Do you want a 'formal' wedding, in a church, with attendants, a reception, music and all the 'trimmings'?"

"I had not even thought about it, Frank. Like most young girls I probably thought of it and even talked about it as my friends and I saw weddings. But after you and I met, all I thought about was being with you. I'm beginning to understand the mother of a bride struggling with all the arrangements telling her daughter, 'just go ahead and elope. Tell us when you get home'. "

"Jayme, we want our wedding to be a happy event. One we will cherish for the rest of our lives. One that our relatives and friends will enjoy. I don't think running down to the court house, getting a license then finding a justice of the peace to marry us fits those requirements. Let's enjoy being together and let the Lord guide us. The next year, while not set in concrete is rather well scheduled."

"You are so wise, Frank. That's another reason I love you. To add fire to the furnace or in this case, to add cold water on a wedding now, some one gave me this magazine. Whoever it was may have been trying to tell us something. Look at this headline, 'Persons marrying before age 25 face a 90% chance of divorcing within two years.' That would not happen to us, but it is a tragedy to those it does."

"Frank, would you go with me and talk to Coach Betty? I'm sure she likes us, and would be honest with us. We don't have to follow her suggestions, but we can put them in our library of ideas."

"Good idea, Jayme. She knows us and she has a petty good idea of what we face in the next year or two."

We were able to set up an appointment with Coach Betty later in the week. As we walked into her office she invited us to sit where we all faced each other and the desk was not between us. A comfortable way to be greeted.

"We have a question, one that does not pertain to basketball. It really does indirectly. Frank and I needed to talk with some one who would be objective and who we admire and respect her opinion."

"It is an honor to be considered under those conditions. I'll bet is about your wedding."

"Yes, it is. Not the wedding itself. Jayme and I are concerned about the timing. We would love to get married tomorrow—at least by next week. We believe we are meant to be together. It is not a question of 'if' but 'when.' Now we are beginning to get hints, some subtle, and some not so subtle, that we should wait until our education is complete, and we have time to 'build' a marriage. These first two weeks under our summer schedule is showing us that we have a lot on our plate."

"Yes, you do. And I want Jayme to be available to work with our team as much as she can. An hour a day beginning this summer, if possible. It is interesting that you come to me with a 'timing' problem. I lost my first love because I insisted on getting our education first. We were in love and he wanted to get married within a week. Time has proven me right. He found a woman who also wanted to get married now. They were married, and within a year they divorced. I can also tell you of friends who didn't wait and who have a wonderful marriage. I wish I could tell you what would be best for you. I can't because no one knows the future. I can see that you will be very busy with sports and academics this coming year. With three years of law school beyond next year, building a solid marriage will have to fight to be heard."

"Coach, we often see you, your husband and your children in church Sundays. Do you believe that God could make our early marriage work?"

" Oh, yes, He could, and would if it fit His life plan for both of you. I have to remind myself that Jesus often asked a recipient of a miracle to do some thing. He told the blind to go and wash in the pool. He may be telling you, "I have something better for you if you complete what I have already given you."

Frank and I sat soaking up what a friend had shared with us. A friend who obviously wanted the best for us and who had already traveled the road on which we were looking. Frank took my hands in his and looking into my eyes asked,

"Jayme, will you accept with me the decision to delay any consideration of marriage until this time next year and maybe until after law school?"

"Yes, I will Frank. I think that is best for us now. And I will promise to cultivate our love for the future."

Thanking Coach Betty for being our friend, and for being such a good listener, we walked slowly out into the garden area and found a bench. We sat down held hands and quietly reviewed what the past few minutes meant to us. I was comfortable with what we had done. I thanked

Frank for initiating the pledge to "seal" our decision. It told me two things. One, Frank is a 'leader' and two he truly loves me. I want those qualities in the man I spend my life with. We agreed that our sport and academic schedules for the next twelve months were quite inflexible. However, their completion would lead to major milestones in our travel through life. The next one, my admittance to the bar could be pursued with freedom from other deterrents."

I looked at Frank, the man I plan to marry and I reached over and hugged him. He returned the hug.

"Frank, do you realize we just almost committed to waiting four years before we marry? Four years! That seems like a lifetime!"

"Yes, it does, Jayme. But we can be together, and we have to live as the best of friends committed to each other. The Lord just gives us a day at a time, but promises to be with us for the days and years to come."

"Frank, I'm beginning to realize how much time our present commitments will absorb. I like the idea of finding a day each week when we can have some time together. I would like to continue that. Also, can we agree that if either of us sees an hour or two when we will have a break, it's o.k. to call the other one to see if they have a break. And it's o.k. to say 'no, I can't take a break right now'."

"I like that, Darling. One thing I plan to do is call you each morning and say 'good morning. I love you'. That may be all we can handle early in the morning."

"That's a nice idea and I will do my best to be awake and be 'pleasant.'

"Enough talk for now, Sweetheart."

With that Frank reached over and pulled me to his shoulder and I thought how nice that was. Eventually, we realized we were hungry and made our way to a nearby Pizza Hut.

As Frank and I expected the next 12 months were busy ones. I spent at least an hour each day with or basketball squad. Each player showed an interest in being their best. I felt like our first session was good. I thought I gave a good incentive "speech."Coach Betty observed and agreed."

"I assume you all know my name is Jayme. I and several others here today were on the team that won the state championship two years in a row. I will be playing on this year's squad. Hopefully, as point guard. I was privileged to be on a state championship team in middle school and in high school. Maybe that's the reason Coach Betty asked me to help us get reacquainted with some fundamentals before the season starts. Make no mistake. Coach Betty is THE Coach of this team!"

"How can we win a game? By putting more points on the board than our opponent? Right?""How can we earn points? By putting the ball through the opponent's goal,"replied one of our seniors. "How else can we increase our score,"I asked. Silence.

"That's right. There is only one way. We can prevent the other team from scoring but that doesn't put points on our score. So our objective through out the game is to put the ball through the opponent's goal. How can we do this?"

"Get control of the ball,"from another senior.

"Good! Moving the ball so a player can do a 'lay-up' or take a three-point shot. Which is the most likely to score? The lay-up, right? How many times have you seen pros, have an open lay-up and miss it?"

Then followed a short session in physics. "Put a spin on the ball and memorize the spot on the glass you should always hit. Take the rest of our hour today perfecting those two actions. Please don't be a show-off, but learn to make these shots EVERY time. I will practice with you because I don't want to miss either. Coach Betty will be most unhappy if any of us miss an easy lay-up. I know some of you are good with a 3-point shot but today let's nail down our skill with the lay-up."

I caught up with Frank as he was waiting at the entrance of the cafeteria. We exchanged 'sweetheart' greetings and got in line for some food.

"How did practice go, Jayme?"

"Good, I thought. Most of last year's players were present and participated in our drill of lay-ups. We started acting like state champions, which we plan to be. How was your day?"

"O.K. I thought maybe I was still in pre-med. My first course is in anatomy. It doesn't seem as detailed and we don't have to memorize all the small bones and how to spell them. Could we go to the library after we eat? I need to do some studying."

"That's a good idea. I need to review my notes from my psychology class."

This proved to be a convenient arrangement many days. We could always use our cell phones to stay in touch. The basketball squad was shaping up nicely. We continued to stress scoring, and the players continued to improve. We started practicing some basic plays. The players from last year's team were very helpful in bringing the new ones into their style of play.

Frank and I managed a visit to one of our homes for special days like birthdays, and of course, Thanksgiving and Christmas. On one weekend we talked my family into letting Frank and I play like we were the host and hostess. We planned the meals, cooked them, cleaned up the house, put the laundry together and did all the things we could think off that we might have to do after we are married. Mother and Dad were excited to watch us and Ken tolerated us. It was a fun thing to do and an education, also.

The school year fell into a routine. Our basketball team became better and better. We easily won our first three games. Coach Betty continually challenged us to be better. I loved working with her. More and more she was letting me select plays on the court. Also, one of our players was developing into a 'natural' at point guard so we let her play as much as we could as she could be my replacement next year. I still loved to play and Coach Betty left me in especially, if we were struggling to stay ahead. I believed our team could easily be a strong contender for state champion.

Frank's classwork kept him busy and his lab classes were mostly with the university's teams. We kept our weekly 'date' and sandwiched a few times in between often in the library. Both of us had spent time with our counselors, and had our schedules written and finalized for the 12 months when I would complete work for my Batchelor's degree, and Frank would get certification as a physical education specialist.

In April, I noticed an announcement of the university's orchestra's spring concert.

"Let's go hear it. It will bring back memories to both of us. Did you say you played the trumpet in high school?"

"Yes, I did and I still have my trumpet. Will our schedules let us take a break and go?

" Sure, and we deserve a change."

The orchestra was good and it did bring back memories of high school. One number on the program was a stirring march. At the appropriate time in the song, I 'mouthed' the drum roll and the roll-of and Frank imitated the trumpet. If the folks around us noticed, they were polite and didn't make fun of us.

"If we just had a vocalist we could go on the road. I think we could make a 'one night stand' if our families would be our audience. "

This new found mutual interest opened another area of our lives together. Frank brought his CD player and we gradually accumulated a music library.

"Good morning, Frank. Are you where you can talk without Jayme listening to our conversation?"

"Yes, mother. I'm in my apartment alone."

"Do you have a ring for Jayme?"

"No, we decided we would save that expense."

"Thinking about it, I remembered we have a ring that originally was my grandmothers. I took it out of the safety box and it is in perfect condition. Bob and I have talked about it and he wants you, as 'senior son' to have it for Jayme, if you want it as an engagement ring. At the appropriate time, you and Jayme can select wedding bands."

"What an unselfish thing for Bob to do. I'll bet Jayme will be thrilled to have the ring. Jayme and I plan to be home for Thanksgiving, would that be a suitable time to give it to her?"

"I think that would be fine. I understand that we will be at Jayme's house for Thanksgiving. I'll have the ring checked to be sure the settings are firmly in place and that it is cleaned."

"Thank you, Mother and Bob. I'll do my best not to tell Jayme our secret before our visit on Thanksgiving. It wont be easy but I'll try."

Frank and I arrived at my house Thanksgiving Day early

(for us). Frank seemed more excited than usual. Mother Johnson and Bob were already there. We had hardly greeted each other when Frank asked if his mother and Bob could have a 'conference'. I was busy helping Mother get last things ready for dinner. It just a few minutes, Frank asked me to see a surprise he had for me. Taking my hand, he held out a jewelry box with the most beautiful ring I had ever seen.

"Darling, will you accept this family heirloom as a token of our engagement to be married. You will be the third generation to wear this ring that was first worn by my great grandmother."

"It will be a joy and a privilege to accept it and cherish it as a token of our promise to be wed."

"Mother remembered the ring and Bob said he would yield to the 'senior son', so I could give it to you."

There followed hugs all around as the beauty of the ring was admired and tears of joy streamed down my face.

Days became weeks, weeks became months and at our Christmas celebration with our families the year before I was to complete law school, I realized we could start wedding plans.

"Frank, let's talk about wedding plans. I will finish law school in June and we probably should set a date so we can tell our families, locate a place and do the little things that make it the happy event we have been dreaming about the past 'hundred years'."

"I'm ready Sweetheart. Do you have a calendar for next year?"

"Yes, I do. My last time at law school is June 1. We can schedule our wedding any time after that and would be free to go on our honeymoon. We are going to have a honeymoon, aren't we?"

"Of course we will. I don't have a place in mind just so you are there. We could even do it in my apartment, but it would be fun to go to some romantic place."

"O.K. my last day in law school is on a Friday. Do we want to schedule our wedding on the following Sunday or do you like a Saturday?"

"I don't have a preference, but the sooner the better."

"Let's bounce the Saturday date on our families and see what happens. Gather around folks, we have an announcement! We think we will have our wedding at three o'clock, June 2, at our church here in my home town. Any questions?"

"What year?" from Bob.

"Next year that's the next June, isn't it?" replied Frank.

The date was acceptable and then followed the usual questions. Will it be a big wedding? Who will you have for brides' maids? Where are you going on your honeymoon? Will there be a reception after the ceremonies? Will you invite many guests?

"Frank and I want a simple ceremony that is exciting, meaningful, includes our families and are brief with only the essential formality. Where we go on our honeymoon, Bob is our secret."

"I want you as my best man, Bob. And you may wear a suit," contributed Frank. "Maybe Ken, will be an attendant to keep Bob in line?"

"Do either of you Moms have a wedding dress that would fit me?

"You might be able wear mine with a few alterations," responded Mother. "It is sealed in a bag hanging in our hall closet. Let's get it out after dinner and see what needs to done to make fit you."

From Mother Johnson: "You are taller than I was when I was married and you are broader across your shoulders. If your mother's wont do we can see what mine looks like. Mine is not unusual in design."

Mother's dress was beautiful and I could squeeze into it. A minor lengthening of the waist and it would fit perfectly.

"Thank you, Mother. I will love wearing it and if Frank and I have a daughter she might wear it."

"I think I will ask my brides maids to chose there own dresses –- something they like and could be worn on other occasions. Frank, I think I will ask Coach Betty to be my matron of honor and Alice and Jean can be brides' maids. If Pastor Williams will conduct the ceremony we've got the wedding party named. Contacting those involved, we found each one pleased to be a part of this wonderful event. Coach Betty (Mrs. Charley Dobson) expressed honor at being asked to be my matron of honor.

A development came to light as we were making last minute arrangements at my house that was great but a complete surprise. We had heard Bob playing with his guitar but when we started listing, he was pretty good. When Ted provided singing we were really impressed.

"When did you guys start performing?"asked Frank.

"Oh, we have working on our act for the past few years,"they replied.

"We don't have any music scheduled for our wedding how about doing a number for us?"I added.

"Sure, we can do that. What song would you like?"

"How about 'Because' or 'Let Me call You Sweetheart,'"suggested Frank.

"Let us work on those two and see what we can do."

If that wasn't surprise enough, when Alice and Jean arrived we heard the four practicing "Because." They were good! And they added music to our wedding.

Frank and I spent our time telling each other how much we loved each other, and how exciting is to anticipate being together completely. We also gave   attention to completing necessary academic tasks.

The thirty six months that three years ago seemed like an eternity were nearing an end. Our basketball team won the state championship with none other than Jennifer my replacement at point guard and captain of next year's team, making the winning basket with a 'driving' lay-up.

In celebration of the outstanding record of the basketball program, the university sponsored a banquet for the players and coaches. Player's families were invited and several came. Mother and Dad would not have missed it. Many individuals were recognized including Coach Betty. Jennifer was asked to make a special presentation. Taking the microphone Jennifer asked me to come to the platform. She had a plaque to present to me.

"I want to read this plaque,

"To Jayme, our assistant Coach, a great player and a wonderful friend. Thank you for your time and your love and a state championship three years in a row. May the Lord continue to bless you as you move on in life's journey. Will the sunshine always be in your heart and the wind at your back."

Signed by all the players and Coach Betty.

I was thrilled and thanked Jennifer and all my teammates,

Coach Betty and all who had made my career exciting and joyful.

"Most of you know that I will have a partner in life's journey, another great basketball player, Frank Johnson."

I was invited to participate in graduation ceremonies although I would not receive my diploma until after summer school. The paperwork for my entry into law school had been completed. Frank received his certification as physical therapist, and the university hospital offered him a place on its staff. Dorms at the university were no longer available to him, so he found a small efficiency that he could rent and it became a convenient place for me to visit with him. The law school provided a dorm for me."

"Do you have a dream, Frank? A place you want to see or maybe an activity to want to be a part of?"

"No, Jayme. My goal now is to spend my life activities with you and our family. I want to be able to provide the needed material things and be your 'soul-mate.'"

"Thank you, Frank. I plan to be there with you. You have read about or have heard of the 'healing power' of associating with an animal. My dream involves horses. I would love to have a place where you and I could have a combination house and office and a place to keep one or maybe two horses. I would bring children who have closed their mind to the world around them, and let them touch and eventually ride a horse. This will enable them to regain the ability to accept their surroundings and enjoy life. It is being done. There are groups who work together and see that this service is available. It may take years to achieve this dream but it has been is in my mind since childhood."

"Yes, Jayme. I have heard of such a program. I believe it is real. May I join you in your dream?"

"Welcome, there is plenty of room. It is now OUR dream."

The wedding was beautiful and meaningful! Frank and I have completed our education, and have established our position in our professions. Our lives are exciting and our love grows stronger each day. Jayda, age four and George, age two have joined our family. After passing the bar exam I was employed by a large law firm, but I soon knew that I would only be a "happy"lawyer if I could have my own practice. I wanted to be with people and to help them in any way that I could. We were working on plans for that combination house and office that is part of our dream. We think we have located the place where we want to build.

PART 2

Jayda

The Joy of Healing Featuring Jayda and Star

There was a rodeo in town and we all went to see the horses, and maybe watch a few events. As Mother and I were walking by the horse barn, the actions of a man about fifty yards ahead of us caught our attention. The man was trying to get a beautiful brown filly into his trailer. He was whipping and cursing the animal. The filly was not cooperating, and the man continued to beat it with a whip, and then with a heavy stick. As the man reached for a bigger whip, the filly broke away and ran to Mother and me stopping and standing beside me. Instinctively, Mother said "Talk to her, Jayda." I did and the horse put her nose on my shoulder. The man walked up still holding the heavy whip.

"Do you have some magic with horses? That mean filly seems to like this little girl. You want to buy that contrary horse for her?"

"How much?" Mother asked without thinking.

"One hundred dollars and she's yours."

"Do you have any papers on her?"

"Yes, I have a big envelope I haven't opened yet. I know she comes from a famous line of quarter horses."

Just then a man walked up to us.

"Any problem, Jayme? I was a judge at the barrel race when you set the world record so I recognized you."

"Do you know this man?"

"Yes, I do. His name is J.B. Smith from Evansville."

"He says he will sell this filly to me for my daughter. The filly who seems to have found a friend."

"May I look in the filly's mouth, Mr. Smith?"

"Help yourself. She's a mean one."

With me holding her, she willingly let our friend examine her mouth.

"Would she let you walk her a few steps away from me?"

"I think so. Come on Star."

No problem. The filly walked away and I turned her around and walked back. Just then Dad joined our little group. Mother introduced Dad.

"Frank, this is J.B. Smith, owner of this filly. The other gentleman was a judge when I won the barrel race many years ago."

"You want the filly?" asked Mr. Smith. "I need to get on the road."

Mother's eyes met those of the judge, and he nodded affirmative.

"Frank, have we got a hundred dollars between us?" Between them they did have one hundred dollars.

"Get me that big envelope, and I will scratch out a

Bill of Sale. Maybe our friend the judge will witness our signatures."

Mr. Smith returned with the envelope which did hold the necessary papers for the filly. Mother counted out the hundred dollars and Mother and Mr. Smith signed the bill of sale. Mr. Smith thanked us and went on his way.

"Mrs. Johnson you are a good horse trader. That filly is easily worth a thousand dollars, and she obviously has found a friend. C.B. Smith is noted for mistreating his animals. Jayda, I look forward to seeing you in a barrel race and for you to beat your mother's world record."

"Thank you, Judge, for being here when we needed you. Some time I will fill you in on the rest of the dream that took a major leap towards fulfillment today."

"Well, here we are Frank, with a beautiful filly, a newly discovered skill of our daughter and no vehicle to transport the filly home. And really no place to keep her at our house. I wonder what Dad is doing this afternoon. I'll call him and find out."

"Hello, Dad. Where are you?"

"Right now I am in the parking lot at the stock show. Where are you and Frank?"

"We are on the stock show grounds near the horse barn. You wouldn't by chance have the horse trailer with you, would you?"

"As a matter of fact, I do. I needed new tires and they had the best deal here. Why do you ask?"

"Dad, would you drive over here by the horse barn—and bring the horse trailer with you? We'll explain when you get here. Thanks."

"Frank, isn't it exciting to see how the Lord puts all the pieces together?"

Grandpa drove up with the horse trailer which my new filly eyed suspiciously. But I spoke to her and it was alright. We filled Grandpa in with the details of the afternoon. He admired the filly and especially how it responded to my directions. He knew of C. B. Smith and his reputation with animals. He also knew the judge whose name was J. K. Russell. Grandpa remembered him as the judge for the barrel race in which Mother set a world record He and Grandpa talked about the filly which I was already calling "Star."

Grandpa had a halter and a short 'lead' in his truck. Properly fitted on Star, he and Judge Russell wondered how Star would slow trot. It would show how she carried herself, and if she walked straight with all four legs.

"She'll show you. How far do you want her to trot? "I asked.

Taking the lead rope, I said, "Come on Star." Star responded by going with me 20 or 30 yards. Turning around to come back, Mother said,

"Give her a little more rope, Jayda and let her chose her pace."

"I did and as we came to where they were all standing, Grandpa and Judge Russell could not stop admiring the filly, and her willingness to follow my simple directions."

"Jayda, I've changed my mind. I'll give you two thousand dollars for Star."

"Sorry, she's not for sale, Judge."

"Keep that answer for anyone who offers to buy Star. She will give you many years of fun and learning. You have a natural gift to communicate with her."

Grandpa added, "Perhaps it's inherited. Jayme had and still has that indiscernible sense to understand a horse."

"Can Star 'board' with you until we can make other

arraignments, Dad? I'm sure Jayda wants to go home with you now. "

"Can I Mother? I need to be sure she finds her new home and is comfortable there. I'll be home in time for school Monday.

"Yes, Jayda you need to help your grandfather show her a nice home."

"O.K. Jayda. Let's see what Star thinks about riding in a good trailer. We'll stop at the supply barn and get a bale of clean straw. She might even like some hay."

"I think I should let her get a drink before we load."

Without hesitation, Star followed me into the trailer where I tied her rope to the bar at the front of the trailer. Backing out of the trailer, I explained to Star that I could not ride in the trailer with her, but would be in the truck pulling the trailer. Grandpa, Star and I made the trip home without incident. Star seemed to approve of the clean stable and a pasture to run in. She wanted me to help her with anything new.

Driving home from the stock show, George had a new computer game and I have been told that Dad and Mother talked about the new situation in our family. That house-office combination and a place for a horse took on new urgency. They knew every thing was o.k. when they drove to pick me up for school and I was out in the pasture riding Star bare-back. A few weeks later, a barrel race track was laid out and I began leading Star on the pattern for the race around the barrels.

I am now eight going on fifteen. My 'Little' brother George is two years younger but shares time riding Star. Our family is living in our combination house and office and the site includes a small pasture large enough for a barrel race layout. Mother and Dad's professional careers are moving forward as fast as they like. Their decision several years ago to get their education before marriage must really have been God's plan for He blesses each day with wonderful, fulfilling love. Mother's dream to work with horses is partially complete ,and the next episode will move it a step closer to fulfillment.

Mother and I were in the room Mother calls her office, and she was busy with "lawyers work"when the door bell rang. I went to the door and it was Lucille Gilbert and her daughter Joyce. I knew Mrs. Gilbert was a client of Mother but I had not met her daughter.

"Joyce and I just came by to tell you I finally settled with the insurance company, and think we are through rounding up all of my assets. Thank you for your help, Jayme."

During their conversation, I noticed that Joyce was giving special attention to the photos of Star which we had on the wall. Also, the bronze replica of a horse that Mother had on her desk seemed to have her special attention.

"Do you like horses, Joyce?'

She nodded her head but didn't say anything.

"Would you like to see my horse?'

Again, she nodded her head and I reached over, took her hand and said,

"Let me show her to you. She's just outside."

Joyce willingly went with me.

"I have one more telephone call I need to make then your mother and I will join you at the corral. You might like to go with the girls, Lucille."

When Mother and Mrs. Gilbert joined us, Joyce was

petting Star and I was showing her how to let Star take a 'treat' from her hand.

"Do you want to work with Joyce, Mother?"

"You are doing great., but I would love to help."

Taking the lead rope , Joyce and I walked Star around a few yards and back to the stand Frank had built to make it easier to get on Star's back.

"Have you ever sat on a horse's back, Joyce?"

"No, I haven't. Can you just sit there?"

"Yes, you want me to show you?"

Joyce nodded and I climbed on Star's back.

"Would you like to sit up here with me?"

"Would Star let me?"

"She won't mind. She likes children to ride on her".

"Give me a boost, Mother."

It didn't surprise me that Joyce was finding this new experience, especially on a horse, different and a bit exciting. My judgment and intent was to move slowly and take Joyce one step at a time.

At first I kept my arm around Joyce, and showed her how to hang on to Star's mane. We walked a few yards, and then I let Joyce take the reins with me. I continued to talk to Joyce and she began to respond.

"Joyce has not said a word since her father died. This is a miracle,"commented Mrs. Gilbert.

When star and I came back to where Mrs. Gilbert was standing, she reminded Joyce that it was time to go to her grandmother's house for supper.

"Do we have to go now, Mother? Star likes me."

"Maybe you can come again, Joyce, but we don't want to keep Grandma waiting."

"Speaking to Joyce, I said I'll show you how to get down.

Hang on to Star's mane, swing your right leg over Star's back and just slide down. Watch me."

No problem. Joyce slid down and reached up and patted Star's neck,

"Thank you, Star. Good bye."

Later that evening Lucille called, and said Joyce hasn't stopped talking all evening. Thank you, Jayda and Star and for doing what no one else could do.

"Some times an animal takes their mind into new territory and starts them on a new adventure. We are so glad it seems to have worked for Joyce."

Mother was excited about the experience with Joyce. She thanked me for working so skillfully with Joyce. It was a thrill yet humbling for her to watch her childhood dream unfold. Another conformation was not long in coming.

I told Mother about a boy in my class who was most unhappy. He was an adopted child, and he had not accepted that as being good. He completed his classwork, but did not participate in school activities or even visit with other students. I made it a point to talk with him about Star and he seemed interested. He even asked if he could see Star. I said he could if it was alright with his parents.

"Was that o.k., Mother?"

"Yes, it was Jayda. That was a nice thing to do. Let's call his mother and see if she agrees. What's the boy's name?"

"It's Roger Potter. Here's his phone number."

When Mother got Roger's mother on the phone she told her that her daughter, Jayda had told Roger he could see her horse Star if it was alright with you.

"Thank you, Mrs. Johnson. My husband and I would love to have Roger see Star. He is having a difficulty adjusting to school and this might help. When is a good time for us to visit? I know where you live and we can make time available when it is convenient with you."

"We are quite flexible. Let me check with Jayda's schedule. (pause) She said this Saturday morning would be fine. Is ten o'clock o.k.?"

"Good. We will see you then. You and your husband and Roger are most welcome."

(Mother to herself, 'another step in my dream'!)

Around our dinner table Mother shared her dream with our family – the first time with George and me. Then I told about my conversation with Roger Potter, and that he was coming to see Star Saturday morning.

Mother suggested that we not make this a "Big Deal", but let the Lord make this His event. We were all welcome to be a part of it, but Mother thought it should be my joy to show Roger what a great horse Star is. We had no idea how Roger would react. He might even be afraid of Star or he may want to sit on her with Jayda. Mother said that I would know. We can be helpful if she asks. My guess, and my prayer, is that Roger will love meeting Star. Probably an hour is long enough for his first visit.

"Mother, how do I show Star to Roger?"

"It will come to you. It might be good to remember Roger probably has never been this close to a horse, and it will be rather big – taller than he is. He may need to learn that it's o.k. to touch him. You might let Star eat a treat out of his hand. Roger will watch you, and anything you do he will tend to copy. If you think he wants to sit on Star, invite him to sit in the saddle in front of you. You can talk to him, answer his questions. You will know how much he wants or needs to know. I will encourage his father or mother to participate by touching Star and maybe lead her if it seems o.k.. Basically, this is yours, Roger's and Star's show. I'm very proud of you, Jayda. You have a gift of knowing people and horses."

A few minutes before ten the Potters arrived. After introductions, I said,

"Come on Roger and meet Star, the greatest horse in the world."

Taking Roger's hand I walked him over to Star who was standing just inside the corral. Typical of Star, she nuzzled Roger for treat. I handed one to Roger and he let Star take from his hand.

"How did you teach her to take a treat from your hand without biting your hand?"

"She just knows how to use her lips and tongue to get the treat. She likes the attention, too."

"How do you ride her?"

"Let me show you. I think you are tall enough. Just put your left foot in the stirrup, like this. take hold of the saddle horn, put your weight on your left foot in the stirrup and pull yourself up in the saddle. Watch me. Now you try it. That wasn't hard was it. Now I'm going to get in the saddle behind you and show you how to guide Star. See these two straps? One is fastened to the left side of Star's bridle—that's what we call the leather harness on her head. The other strap is fastened to the right side of the bridle. Now take one strap in each hand like this. What do you tell Star if you want her to go?"

"Gidd ep."

"Yes, that is the usual word used. But you could say 'go, Star.' She will respond to your tension on the reins. If you let them be quite loose or even shake them gently, she will get the idea. Suppose you want her to stop, what would say and how would you hold the reins?"

"Whoa, and tighten the reins"

"Very good. How would you tell Star to turn to the right?"

"Pull on the right rein; to the left pull on the left rein."

"Now drive Star around the corral."

Roger was soon driving Star all around the corral. "Now talk to her, Roger as you want her to change directions."

."It doesn't matter very much what words you use. You might say, Star, 'turn left, Star, or good girl , Star"

"Jayda, does Star have a mother and father?"

"Yes, she does ,but we don't who they are. Would you like to hear the story of how Star came to live with us?"

"Yes, I would."

"We were all at the stock show and Mother and I were near the horse barn. The man who owned Star was trying to get her in a trailer. He was whipping her and beating her. Star broke loose from the man and she came over and stood by me. The man came over where we were and asked Mother, "You want to buy the filly for your daughter?"They agreed on a price and Star came to live with us. She seemed glad to have a clean stall and a pasture to run in. She and I have become good friends

I drove Star to where Mother was standing with Roger holding the reins.

"I'm going to slide off, Roger and then you get off. You remember how to do it."

"Sure, just like you showed me."Grabbing the saddle horn, Roger swung his right foot over Star's back and slid down beside me. Patting Star, he said, "thank you Star."

"Mom, Dad that was great and you know what? Star was adopted too. Look how happy she is."

Just then George showed up with a base ball and invited Roger to join him, which he did.

"Thank you, Jayda. You may have encouraged Roger to be himself. How did you know to tell him Star was adopted?"

"He asked me if Star had a mother and father. I told him yes, but we didn't know who they were. Then I told him how Star came to us and is ours. She seems happy with her new home and she loves to have children talk to her and feed her and keep her stall clean. Roger did not comment so I guess that answered his question."

"This is the first time he has come out of his 'shell', commented his father. " We have taken him to doctors, psychologists, our pastor but no one seemed to reach him. In less than an hour, you have done what others could not do. Thank you."

Mother added: "For some reason, some animals give a child or an adult the reason or ability to reach the mind. It is exciting to see it happen."

"How much do we owe you for this visit Mrs. Johnson?"

"There's no charge. We have enjoyed what seems to be a step forward for Roger. Jayda is the key to what has happened. First, she sensed that Roger needed a friend, and as we had talked about how animals sometimes help, she suggested that Roger might like to see Star. Then she had the wisdom to move slowly. She and I talked about it briefly, but she knew Roger might even be afraid of Star, After all, she is sort of big."

Just then Frank arrived with cool drinks. Jayda left to play ball with Roger and George. After introductions and exchanging business associations, Mr. Potter said to Frank,

"Did you see how Jayda made Roger feel comfortable with Star?"

"Yes, I did but it was what I expected. She has a rare ability to sense people and horses feelings. Roger appears to have unused talents, but he is doing good with a base ball."

Mother shared her dream with the Potters, and they discussed tentative plans for forming a nonprofit organization and seeking grants and support for such an operation.

"You and Roger have reassured me that my dream is needed and is feasible. The Lord has lead Frank and I through so many situations that led to joyful experiences so I am sure He will continue to show us the way. I can visualize hundreds of children finding their way through such a program."

"Thank you for sharing your dream with us. We believe the Lord led us to you, and we will join you in prayer for God's leadership as His will becomes a reality in the lives of those in need."

Word of Roger and my event with Star soon became well known in our community. Other parents called to see if their child could see Star. Our schedules did not give us time to properly repeat the event for a few weeks.

Mother had an interesting experience that did not involve me but was important in the development of her dream. One day she received a phone call.

"This is Jayme Johnson. How may I help you?"

"This is Sarah Higgins. You do not know me, but I have heard of the wonderful experience Roger Potter had with your daughter and her horse, Star. I work with a group that tries to use animals to help children overcome handicaps, physical and mental."

"I'm so glad to talk with you. I knew there were others

who believed as I do, that such an encounter can often break barriers that other treatments have been unsuccessful in treating. I would love to meet your group. Would it be possible for its members to meet at our place? You could meet my husband who is a physical therapist and also, Jayda and Star. We could make it a picnic if that would be interesting to your group."

Following this conversation, Mother and I found a date the group could meet at our house, and a picnic was accepted with pleasure. Thus, began a relationship that was fun and helpful to all of us. Our guests were properly impressed with my ability to work with Star.

There followed a discussion of ways to make this treatment available, and means of financing such a program. Mother's work in law had not brought her in contact with nonprofit organizations. A call to a fellow attorney who did work with nonprofits, convinced her group it should investigate this area of financing. When she told her fellow attorney about our experiences, he offered to meet with us and explain some of our options. Mother thanked him and set up a tentative date for a meeting.

Two attributes of a nonprofit organization were of special interest to me and Mother. One, they could accept grants from both public and private groups, and second they were exempt from Federal and most state income taxes. Officers and directors of the organization could not receive any income from the organization. However, they could employ persons to do work for the group, and they could be paid a reasonable wage or salary.

Mother agreed to serve as chairman of five to work with a fellow attorney—whose name is Leonard Shaw – and outline steps that we would need to take to have a nonprofit.

If Mother had known the amount of time this would require she might have declined. But it could provide a permanent device to give her dream a life of its own.

The committee learned that there were several ways of financing a program. Some people simply charged a fee and made it a part of their other business activities. Still others helped clients file a claim with their health insurance company. Only one group that we heard about had formed a nonprofit company. It had just started so it was not much help.

The committee's report suggested charging a fee, and working with insurance companies to secure reimbursement for clients. It suggested further study of the use of a nonprofit organization. The ability to accept grants was a strong factor. Plus, providing some continuity to the program.

Star and I continued to work with some children but I was becoming more and more involved in school and its activities, and had less time to work with children and Star.

Time to fast forward again.

My twelve birthday has come and gone. I have been watching some rodeos on TV, and Star and I am ready to run a barrel race. We have been running the pattern in our pasture consistently under 15 seconds. One day there was an announcement of a barrel race at the rodeo that was coming to town. Dad and Mother asked me if I really wanted to run in the race.

"Star and I are ready," was my emphatic reply. Dad got the entry forms and sent them to San Antonio. Star and I really got serious about training, and made several runs under Mother's old record of 14 seconds. Grandpa brought his horse trailer, and we loaded up for the trip to San Antonio and the rodeo. What memories flooded through Mother's mind as she`recalled a similar trip a generation ago with her horse named Star.

Unloading at the horse barn we were pleased to see Judge Russell. He greeted us warmly, and told me he had been expecting me and Star. My race would be in the morning and Judge Russell promised to be there as he expected me to beat Mother's record. Mother was pleased to know that I might very well dethrone her. Who better to do it than her own daughter?

I was number three in the line for the race. Star and I were not concerned as we talked about the race. I talked and Star listened. We were announced and off we went. It felt like a good race."

"My equipment must have malfunction,"announced the time keeper. "I got a time of 13.9 seconds which is below the record run."

"I don't think it malfunctioned,"answered Judge Russell. "Several of us with stop watches timed the run in fewer than 14 seconds."

This called for a conference with Dad, Judge Russell and I participating.

"You already have a record run,"mentioned Dad.

"How critical is the time-keepers report?"he asked.

"It could lead to a dispute,"admitted Judge Russell. "Suppose Jayda makes another run, and we agree that the best run of the two would be the official run."

"If it would be better, Star and I don't mind running again. But things can happen. Can I have it in writing that my best time in either run will be official?"

"I'll put it in writing,"answered Judge Russell.

Mother's law degree raised its flag and she asked,

"Do you have authority to bind the Rodeo?"

"I am a director of the Stock Show and Rodeo and 'yes' I can bind the rodeo and the barrel race."

"O.K. Jayda, what's your decision?"

"As my attorney, Mother. I'll go with you. Come on Star. Let's show them how this race is supposed to be run."

Star and I walked a few yards then I signaled that we ready. Judge Russell to time keeper:

"Get that gadget of yours ready because this is going to be another record."

Star and I took off like winners. We ran the pattern and when we started for "home"I had to grab the saddle to keep from falling backwards, Star took off so fast. Cheers roared at the finish line as it was obvious that it was a record run.

From the timekeeper:"my equipment worked perfectly. Time: thirteen point eight ,five seconds!"

What a thrill for Mother to see me, her daughter, break her record! I was deluged with congratulations and comments on the action of Star. At one point, a man approached me and wanted to buy Star. I gave him the answer I had given to Judge Russell earlier; "She is not for sale."

The gentleman went over to talk to Mother.

"I understand you are the mother of the young lady who just set a new record in the barrel race."

"Yes, I am the very proud mother of Jayda. She just broke my old record of 14 seconds which I made nearly twenty years ago."

"Mother, this man wanted to buy Star. I told him she was not for sale."

"I didn't mention a price,"contributed the gentleman,

whose name was Sam. "I will pay ten thousand dollars for that outstanding filly. I'm sure you are involved in her title as this beautiful young lady is still a minor."

"Mother, that is a lot of money do I have to sell her?"

"Jayda, she is your horse. You are the only one who can decide to sell her."

"I'll give you twenty thousand,"interrupted the man.

"Thank you very much. It is exciting to know some one else recognizes what a great horse she is. But my answer still is, she is not for sale. She is a part of me. And I do not want to part with her."

"Here is my card. My offer is good for ninety days. If you change your mind or just want to talk about it, call me."

"Mother, did I do the right thing I asked?"as Dad joined us.

"I heard part of the conversation and I am very proud of you, Jayda. You were every inch a lady. If Star is that valuable we better see about some insurance, and recheck the locks on her stall and the gates to her pasture. There are persons who would steal her and sell her."

A reporter asked Mother, "didn't you run a barrel race also with a horse named Star?"

"Yes, I did and set a world record in this same coliseum and with a horse named Star. What a thrill to see my daughter break my record!

"Was this the same horse that Jayda rode?"

"No, we had to put my horse down soon after we won the race. Her bones began to deteriorate and her right front leg and ankle broke as I was riding her in the pasture. It broke my heart to put her down, but I could not let her suffer. Jayda's Star is no kin of my horse as far as we know."

Sam, who wanted to buy Star, did call a few weeks later, and said he had a idea for me and Star. Here's his suggestion.

"There is a major rodeo in New York City next month, and a barrel race will be a featured event. The purse may exceed one hundred thousand dollars. The publicity for Star and Jayda would be more than any rodeo has seen. If it can be worked out, I will pay all expenses for you, Frank, Jayme and Star to come to New York City, and for you and Star to run in the race. This would include transportation to and from New York City and living expenses while in New York. Winnings would be spilt half to you have to me. I think you, your mother and Star should be in New York City a day before the race. Think about this idea, and call me by this time next week."

"Wow!" was my reaction.

Dad and I got on the Internet, and soon had a tentative budget and time table. Dad checked to be sure the insurance on Star would be valid for such an event. Then he called Mr. Roof (Sam) and they compared budget and timing data. They were pretty much in agreement. Mr. Roof suggested adding 15% to expenses as there always were 'unforeseen ' items.

Now to keep Star healthy and in shape. She loved the additional attention, and I and all my friends were excited. Mr. Roof sent promotional material on the rodeo, and most of a page was devoted to Star and me.

Grandpa was not to be left out, and he volunteered to use his horse trailer and drive to New York City. Grandmother and Dad would ride with him. Mother and I would fly and be in New York City to welcome them. Mother and I located the arena, and were pleased to greet Judge Russell. He would be one of the judges in the barrel race. Mr. Roof was with him so we got all the information about a stable for Star. There was a motor home right on the grounds and a place to park the trailer. Grandpa, Grandmother, Dad and Star arrived late the next day. With our cell phones we were able to direct them to the horse barn. Star was glad to see me, and I walked her and talked to her. My race was not until the next day so we had time to exercise and become familiar with the race area.

The Press learned that Star and I were present, and there was no end of pictures, questions and speculation on what time we would make in the race. Star didn't mind and I "ate it up."

The morning of the race, I was ready. I had been able to find room for Star to 'stretch' her legs and do a few sprints. I felt good about the race. Mr. Roof came by and assured me that this was not a life or death matter. Just run your race and enjoy it. Contestants were allowed one practice run. I decided to do it since Star had not seen this arena, and the crowd would be a little loud. The practice run looked good to Mother. Star seemed to enjoy the crowd.

The first two riders made good runs but their times were between 17 and 18 seconds. I put Star at the starting position and off we went! The turn around the second barrel was a little sloppy but when we swung around the last barrel Star really turned it on! I grabbed the saddle horn and we roared home! Dad and Grandpa raised their hands in the air! Mother's watch showed the time as less than 14 seconds. The scorekeeper:

"Time: thirteen and eight tenths seconds. A new world record beating the record established by Jayda's Mother, and a filly named Star fifteen years ago in this same arena."

Mr. Roof and Judge Russell were the first to congratulate me after Dad and Grandpa. The Press was everywhere shooting pictures and making notes. Mother finally got close enough to grasp my hand and give me a 'high five.' I threw her a kiss.

Some one asked if I would pose on Star one more time. I was pleased to do so. I had a treat in my pocket which I gave to Star as I mounted for more pictures."

Mr. Roof asked if the motor home was satisfactory. We assured him it was very adequate.

"I'll find you in the morning and we will settle our finances. They didn't have a total on the purse, but said it would be over one hundred thousand. What a thrill to see Star and Jayda perform."

I was taking Star for a morning walk when Mr. Roof came to the horse barn.

"Good morning to the world's greatest barrel racer. Are you and Star ready for another race?"

"Give us a few minutes," I responded, "we will be ready."

Mother joined Dad and I and Mr. Roof. After the usual greetings Dad asked if an offer of fresh coffee, and a table to lean on would be in order. Sounded good and I hooked Star's lead on the door to the trailer, and we all found a seat around the table. I chose orange juice instead of coffee.

"The riding skill of Jayda, and her wonderful ability to communicate with Star plus Star's strength and willingness to obey Jayda, was evident when I first saw them race. Yesterday confirmed my judgment. What a show they put on for a record crowd!"exclaimed Mr. Roof.

"The purse for this event also was a record, $124,000. In accordance with our agreement, Jayda's share is $62,000. How would you like to receive it? A check? Cash?"

"Mother, this is your area of expertise and as my attorney, I want your suggestion. Also, could we share the cost of this trip with Mr. Roof? His interest and financial advance has been critical to an experience of my young life."

"Dad would that be o.k. with you?"

"You are right, Jayda. Without his interest and willingness to 'gamble' on the race, it would not have happened. Can you come up with a ball park figure of your expenses, Mr. Roof, or will you need to wait until all your bills get in?"

"Jayda, that is so generous of you but so like you. I don't have all the bills in, Frank, but if Jayda is serious, I will settle for $1,000 as half of my expenses."

"Is that O.K., Jayda? I think that is a reasonable amount."

"Good. Mother, how will you take my money?"

"We have not talked about money, only 'let's win the race.' I'm sure Jayda has a few items she would like to buy. After all, she starts middle school this fall. Here's a suggestion: Make a check for $1,000 payable to Jayda. Being aware that Jayda is a minor, suppose the balance which I think is $61,000, be in a check made payable to Frank and Jayme Johnson, for the benefit of Jayda Johnson, a minor. We can put it in a special account and draw on the account as Jayda needs or wants to spend it."

"Fine. I'll write those checks now. Let's give the banking system ten days to clear these transactions. I will check on this end, and you can let me know if the money isn't in your bank by the end of ten business days."

"It has been fun and profitable to know you. Have a safe trip and Jayda, may I call you if I have another race we could win for the world and us?"

"Yes, my school is taking more and more of my time but call me and we can talk about it. I'm sure Star is ready."

"Are you going to drive home today?"

"No, Jayda has never seen New York City so we plan a quick tour of the city then get an early start tomorrow. Jayme and Jayda have agreed to ride in the truck, so Jayme and I can share the driving. We might go all the way home tomorrow."

The trip home was uneventful. We made a stop in Missouri to let Star stretch her legs and we had a hot meal. Dad and Mother set up my account as planned, and I had a ball spending the thousand dollars. Star might have gotten an extra feeding of oats.

My friends and I were excited about starting middle school. We shopped for clothes, and looked to see what classes we would have together. I decided to continue in the band. I enjoyed playing the clarinet, was told I was a natural for this instrument. I played basketball and volley ball, but music was my love. The band director at middle school was pleased to have me in the band, and expected me to do some solo work.

I was assigned solo parts with the band, and when our church decided to add some instruments to the choir program I became a featured soloist, and traveled with the choir on mission trips. Other instrumentalist joined the choir, but I was the leader of the instrumental group. I did special solos with the choir, and did some composing for the instruments as they supported the choir.

Just before my last year in middle school, I was given a scholarship to attend the prestigious music school in Interlocken, Michigan. I would be one of several hundred students from many states. I might be a guest at the church where my grandmother Goodman and my great grandmother

Moore, attended in Traverse City. They often had students from Interlocken as guests.

I came home all excited about the time at Interlochen. I did visit the church where my grand parents had been members and several remembered Grandmother Goodman. In fact, I was invited to play a solo at one service.

The most exciting experience at Interlocken was meeting a fellow clarinet player. His name is John Goodnight and he loves horses. He is a freshman at San Angelo High School. We composed a duet for our clarinets, and played in the orchestra for graduation. I enjoyed knowing him.

The end of middle school called for parties to celebrate this milestone in a student's journey to adulthood. I remembered hearing about the great party Mother's parents threw for her when she graduated from middle school.

"Can I have a party for some friends to celebrate our jump to high school?"was my question one evening.

"You can have friends over any time, Jayda and we would love to help you have a "graduation"party. How many would you like to invite?"

"Let me start a list."

"Mother, this list just keeps growing. How many can we have in our house without it being too crowded?"

"If we use uncle Ken's idea and use plastic utensils and a buffet we can have as many as can get in the house. Put your list together, and let's see if we have any problems."

It was a great party and almost everyone in my class came. A few would be out of town starting their vacation. At one point during the party, I got out my clarinet, one of the boys from the band had his trumpet, and we soon had a jazz group going. A girl played the piano, one of the drummers found a metal can cover for a drum and we were in business.

At 2:00 A.M. the agreed time to end the party, the group improvised "Auld lang syne"and the party reluctantly came to an end. My parents and I were deluged with thanks for having a party of which all could be proud.

High school was a step up in the educational ladder and grades would now be an official part of each student's scholastic record. This could be important in gaining admittance to some universities and a factor in obtaining scholarships. Grades were not a problem for me. The band was fun, and I quickly learned to play my clarinet and march in the field formations. Composing music for accompanying the church choir was challenging but interesting. The Minister of Music invited me to conduct the choir, but I declined saying I would give my energy to the instrumental section. I often played a solo with the choir. My small "pick up"group enjoyed getting together, and keeping the world of jazz alive and well. By my junior year we had a trumpet, a guitar, a string bass plus my clarinet in our group. We were getting requests to provide music at parties and study groups (Yes, studying was part of the activity). At one "gig"a girl from the choir asked if she could provide the vocal part to one of our jazz pieces. She was welcomed and was good! From then on, the group had a vocal soloist, and we said to ourselves, "we could go on the road."We probably could, but I had my heart set on being a top clarinetist, and continued to polish my skills playing and composing. My scholastic grade level continued above 3.9."

Social activates were an essential part of my life. I had many friends and always had invitations to parties and other fun events. Like most high schools, the junior prom was the top social event of the year. Rumors of who was going with whom floated from room to room, and if you were not going there must be something wrong with you. I had several invitations but had not accepted any. I came home one day and told Mother,

"I have a date for the prom."

"Is it a secret or are you going to share the news with your family?"

"I will be pleased to share it, but I want you to guess who it is."

"You have mentioned several but I'm going for a long shot, Roger Potter?"

"How did you guess, Mother?"

"Just a hunch, but I knew you had been visiting at school and he seemed like a normal person after his session with you and Star. And you had mentioned that he was one who had invited you to the Prom."

"He is a nice person, and we enjoy visiting so I said yes to his invitation. Can we talk about another part of the Prom, Mother?"

"What's this about the Prom? Asked George as he walked into the room. I've heard that several parties are being planned. From what I know about the people planning to host some of them they would be better called a 'drinking party' not an 'after Prom' party."

"I hear the same thing, George. This brings up my other question about the Prom. Mother, I seem to remember stories about an After Prom party that you had at your house when you went to your prom."

"Yes, we did, Jayda. It was hosted by Dad and Mother, and it was the talk of the town. We faced a similar problem with some of parties involving excessive drinking of which we did not want to be a part. It was a fun party, and most of my class attended. Would you like to have an After Prom party at your house?"

"YES, I know several of my classmates would love to have that option. We'll do all the decorating and the cleaning up after the party. Thank you, Mother."

"My turn to bring up memories,"added George. I seemed to have heard that uncle Ken made a suggestion that solved many problems. In case you have forgotten, I will fill in the details."

"You are right, George. Ken did make some suggestions that made it an easy party and we used them all."

"I think we should send invitations so we will know how many supplies we will need. I'll write one on the computer and recheck my list of people who would be interested. What day and what times should I put on the invitations? The last day of classes is Wednesday, May 23rd. Can we try Friday, June 1?"

"That sounds O.K. I think we used thirty minutes before the end of the Prom as the time our house would be open. Breakfast was 4:30 or 5:00 and going home was seven o'clock."

"The Prom is scheduled to close at one o'clock. Most who go will want to stay till the end. Why don't we say one fifteen for the start of our party? We can fill a tub with soft drinks and glasses for ice water and plates of hors d'oeuvres. Breakfast at four o'clock and going home seven o'clock."

"That sounds good, Jayda. Why don't you call two or three of your friends and get their suggestions."

"I know three that will be coming."

"Mother, they were all thrilled about coming to our

house after the Prom. Janet, whose father is a professional photographer, said he would be available to take photos until two o'clock."

"Here's a idea for the invitation. Any suggestions?"

Put A Crown On Your Prom!

"Come to our house after the Prom. My
Father, Mother, George and I will host an
After Prom party!
Here's our planned schedule;
1:00 . . . . .Prom ends
1:15 . . . . .our house opens
'Till 2:00 Photos courtesy Jane's father
4:00 . . . . .Breakfast
6:00 . . . . .Es hora de casa.

Jayda, George, Jayme and Frank Johnson
RSPV so we will have plenty of food
1368 Brookside. 647-0360 or E-mail Jayda.

"I have thirty names on my list. Is that to many, Mother?

"That could mean as many as sixty attending. We could open the patio if it isn't raining."

"I think that would be great,"contributed George." "A crowd is more fun."

"Would it be appropriate for me to invite my friend John and a friend from San Anglo?"He knows I have a date here, but I think he would like to come."

"How would your date react, Jayda? "

"Good question. He knows about my clarinet player

friend. I think John would bring his own date. I'll think about it."

"Invitations were mailed two weeks before the date of the party, and acceptances came rolling in —many by return mail and my email were jammed with replies. A few sent regrets as they would be on vacation. John called and thanked me for including him, and he and a friend would be here."

"What a party! Girls dressed in their elegant party dresses and the guys in formal tux. Couples lined up to have Janet's father take their pictures. With my computer, he was able to print photos immediately, so the photos could be autographed at the party. There soon were lines to get autographs. Everyone wanted my autograph. Several asked Jayme, Frank and George to sign theirs. George was able to find a supply of envelopes so the photos could be safely taken home."

"As uncle Ken suggested a decade ago, breakfast was buffet style, and a hungry group of teenagers soon mixed their conversations with eggs, bacon, sausage, sweet rolls, toast, orange juice and coffee. Five parents had volunteered to help and the party slowly came to an end. By 7:30 all had said goodbye and a million thanks! My "clean up crew" stayed until the house was back to "normal."

"John worked with the clean up crew and as they were finishing, I led him out to the corral to meet Star.

'What a beautiful filly," was his reaction. I introduced Star to John and handed him a treat which Star gladly took from John's hand.

"Could I come when I can be in my riding clothes and ride Star?

"I think that would be nice, and I'm sure Star would enjoy it. You can see we have a barrel race laid out in the pasture, so maybe you could see how good you are with a world record filly."

"Thank you, Jayda. I'll be in touch. The party was great. Thank you for including me. You have the kind of friends I would expect you to have. They're O.K. and so are you."

After school was out, John did call, and set up a time when he could visit. He wore his riding clothes (and brought his clarinet). First item was to reintroduce Star to John. She greeted him like an old friend and John mounted on her. After getting acquainted with a little trotting he let her walk through the barrel race pattern.

"I have a stop watch. See what you can do running the race." Star knew what was expected of her, and she gave John a fast ride. Sixteen seconds. Not bad. See if you can bring it down to fourteen seconds." The next run was fifteen point one seconds."

"Let's see if I can do any better. Mounting my favorite filly, I whispered in Star's ear, 'now show him how it's done.' Taking two strides we crossed the starting line like champions."

"WOW! This stop watch must be off! That was fourteen seconds!"

"We were a little sloppy on the second barrel. But it felt good. Our record was thirteen, point eight."

"I love the way Star responses to directions. By the way, what did you whisper in her ear just before you started?"

"I'm not sure of the words, but it was to encourage her to give it her best. They seem to respond to feelings that the words convey. It is a gift. Possibly an inherited one. Mother has the same ability to communicate with animals. Did I tell you how we happened to have Star?"

"No, I would like to hear that story."

So I told John the story of Star coming to me almost for protection from a "mean"owner, and how Mother without thinking offered the man a hundred dollars for the filly and he accepted it.

"What a story, Jayda! You have a wonderful gift, and it has been validated by the experiences you have told me about with the little girl, and the boy in your class. I met him at the party, and it was obvious that he is very proud of you. We only visited briefly, but being your date for the Prom was the high light of the evening for him."

"We have shared feelings and ideas, so I feel I can ask a very personal question. You can answer, 'none of your business' if you prefer. With the many invitations I'm sure you received, how did Roger win?"

"I don't mind your asking. We have shared many ideas. I really don't know why I accepted Roger's invitation. It wasn't in sympathy thinking no one else might accept it. It wasn't because we had had a special experience. I liked him and he is pleasant company. Maybe subconsciously I wanted to reinforce his acceptance of what life had dealt him. I'm glad you asked, John. Yours and my relationship is on a different level. I enjoy the time we have together."

"Now let's see what the refrigerator will yield in cold drinks and snacks."

"Mother welcomed John back to our house. It's a little quieter than at the Prom party. I think George left some chocolate cake, and you know there's ice cream in the freezer, Jayda."

"It is a pleasure to be in your house again. It was a happy 'after the Prom' party. I wore my riding clothes today so I could get better acquainted with Star. She is a pleasure to ride, and with Jayda to introduce me she was soon my friend."

"Mother, John rode Star around the barrel race pattern in fifteen seconds."

"Then Jayda did it in fourteen seconds. Does she have a secret that she whispers in Star's ear?"

"She and Star do seem to understand each other."

"May I assume you brought your clarinet today? Let's show Mother how good we are. Do you remember our duet?"

"I think so. Start it and I'll see if I can remember my part."

We did remember and even George, who came in when he heard music, cheered when we finished. He brought his stringed bass from his room and added some bass for the jam session that followed.

"John, we haven't talked about colleges. I assume you will be going to Texas A.&M.."

"Yes, that's my plan. Oklahoma has a good Animal Husbandry school, but I think I'll continue the family tradition and be an Aggie. Have you decided where you will go? "

"Not yet. I want to major in psychology with some work in counseling. Texas A.&M. is a possibility. We could be in that great A.& M. band?"

"Can girls be in the band now? For many years band members had to be in the Corps, and girls could not be in the Corps. Times may have changed. They should let girls in the band."

"I might go to the University of Texas. I want to look at its curriculum. Will you be doing any rodeos at A.& M.?"

"I don't think so. I want to get as much accounting as

possible, and hopefully some new tricks in computing that will help me be efficient in ranching. Maybe I can find a group that likes music and can use a good clarinet player. "

"Sounds, like fun, John, we'll see how things work out in the next few weeks. We'll stay in touch."

"Thank you for letting me make a friend of Star. Thank you, Mrs. Johnson for rearing such a beautiful and talented daughter. She is a pleasure to know and fun to visit. We are loading calves in the morning so I better go home. Dad will expect me up at daylight to help. I'll bet Star would be a great horse to ride in a round-up. Bye."

"John is comfortable to be with, Jayda. Has he decided which college he will attend?"

"Yes, it's Texas A. & M. for him. He plans to return to the family ranch, and he said he would perpetuate the family tradition and be an Aggie. He also wants to learn accounting and some more computer programs. These will be increasingly important in the ranching business."

"Have you decided where you want to go?"

"No, Mother I am still thinking. Could we visit some universities in the next few weeks? I know I want to major in psychology and some counseling if possible. I would like to visit Texas A. & M., The University of Texas, and your alma mater. Maybe others. Being at A. & M. with John would be nice."

"What about your music? You know you enjoy it and are very good."

"I love to play my clarinet, and I hope wherever I go there will be an opportunity to play in a band or orchestra. I don't have the passion for a career in music. My dream is more like yours. Helping the handicapped, hopefully with horses. It's so satisfying to see the change that can take place in lives with the little help I can give."

"It is exciting, and thank you, Jayda for wanting to carry the dream forward. Let's see if we can schedule those visits to colleges before Thanksgiving. That will give you time to make applications to your favorites."

Our whole family made Texas A. & M. the last visit to universities the week before Thanksgiving. Completing our tour in the cafeteria we were greeted by John.

"He introduced us to his mother Carolyn, sister, Roselyn and his father Fred. This is the beautiful girl I met at Interlocken, and she plays a 'mean' clarinet and has won many honors with her solo work. More importantly, she is the owner of the wonder filly, Star. I have told you of some of its talents. Would you get your trays and join us?"

"Thank you, we would be pleased to."

There followed a pleasant conversation between two families that would become better known than either expected at that time."

"John, I didn't expect to you on the tour. I thought you had already decided to come here."

"Oh, I had but we thought we would see if they have anything new. And they do—a symphonic orchestra! I have already signed up for a place in the clarinet section. Come join us! We can show them how it should be played! Would you like to meet Dr. Foster the conductor who is also director of the music department?"

"Do we have time, Mother?"

"Yes, take as much time as you like."

When John and I approached the music department we

heard music from the concert hall. Some prospective students were trying out for the orchestra. When the conductor saw John he stopped the playing and greeted John who quickly presented me.

"I heard Miss Johnson play a solo at the concert of the All State orchestra. May I sign you up for our orchestra? We already have John assigned a seat in the clarinet section."

"Thank you, sir. It could be fun. However, I haven't even decided to attend A. & M. My parents and I have been visiting several universities to see which one will give me the curriculum I want. I plan to major in psychology."

"I can understand that. Your work with a young filly, named Star, is well known. You obviously have a talent for working with children and horses. We would love to have you continue to enjoy your music with us."

"Thank you for knowing about Star. She is a sensitive and well behaved filly. You have added a plus for A. & M. I will be making a decision soon."

Returning to their families, John commented that the music director had heard me play a solo and was ready to assign me a seat in his orchestra. He also knew about the wonderful filly named Star.

"Johnson family conference, please. (to my family) This is where I want to go. It seems to offer all I want including an opportunity to keep in touch with my music. Do you agree?"

Even George added his approval. Turning to John and his family, I said "welcome another aggie."

John could not resist giving me a big hug which I welcomed. Thus, began a relationship between two families and two young people that would grow over the years and provide many happy events."

Having made the decision to go to Texas A. & M., I concentrated my efforts to complete my senior year in high school. My contacts with John became more frequent as we discussed college and personal ideas.

Mother received a call from Mrs. Goodnight about a week before Christmas inviting our family to visit them during Christmas vacation.

"We hoped we would have an opportunity to visit before our youngsters go off to college. Our guest cabin easily sleeps eight and it will be available. We want you to have meals with us. Our suggestion is for you to come to San Angelo Wednesday afternoon and spend Thursday and Friday with us. San Angelo is having a rodeo on Thursday and Friday. Some of the rodeo may be interesting. I think John may participate in one or more events."

"That would be fun! I am going to accept with thanks and assume other family members can change their schedules if necessary. Jayda will be thrilled, and George will be excited to visit a real ranch. What a treat for Frank and me to spend some time with you and your family."

I had been outside during the conversation with Caroline. Mother called me and asked me if I would like to visit John and his family at their ranch?

"Can we leave today? What a treat that would be! Are you serious, Mother?"

"Yes, Caroline just called and invited us for two days during Christmas vacation and I accepted for all of us. She said their guest cabin will sleep eight and we would have our meals with them."

YEAH! I've wanted to see their ranch. John brags about how wonderful it is. We can stay two days?"

"Yes, Caroline suggested we drive up Wednesday afternoon and stay through Friday. It's about a three hour drive. Let's tell George and Dad."

Excitement built at both families as the time of the visit neared. Mother and I found an appropriate gift to take to the Goodnights. By lunch time on Wednesday, we were packed ready to go. Arriving at the ranch we were greeted with hugs and typical Texas hospitality. After greetings and putting suitcases in the guest cabin everyone, found a place on the porch of the house which overlooked a small corral and a pasture. The ranch foreman was struggling with a young horse that refused to submit to his commands. I watched this failure of the foreman to make any progress and whispered to John, "could I see if he will respond to my method?"

"Sure, Dad, Jayda wants to try her hand with 'Red.' "

"Do you have a treat—maybe an apple that Red would like? "

With my pocket loaded with apples, I approached Red slowly and quietly speaking to him as I approached him. The rope was still on Red. It is not known what words I used, but I soon had Red eating a treat from my hand. I removed the rope, asked John quietly for a halter then later a bridle, a saddle blanket and to set a saddle near her. In less than thirty minuets, I was in the saddle walking Red around the corral. The observers started to cheer but Mother raised her hand and whispered, "not yet." I brought Red up to John. Talk to him, John. Slowly and softly. Give him a treat and stroke his neck. I'm going to dismount and see if he will let you mount up. In a few minutes, Red did permit John to get in the saddle and they rode around the corral."

"Keep talking to him John and gradually let him has his head. See if he will trot and still leave you in control."

John brought Red up to the porch and Mother and I led a reasonably quiet cheer. John rode around a few minutes then turned Red loose in the corral. Red followed John to the porch where he nuzzled Mother and I then went to the water trough. This performance was not a surprise to the Johnsons. They had seen similar scenes before. The ranch foreman whose name was Joe was beside himself.

"What did you say to that horse, Miss Johnson?"

"Mostly, I just talked. He didn't know what the words meant but he sensed my attitude, and that I wasn't afraid of him and that I liked him. The treat and stroking him helped. Mother, you did a similar thing before I was born. Would you add anything?"

"No, Jayda you have mentioned the critical elements. We must admit that we have a God given ability to sense the feelings of animals especially horses.   It's always a thrill to see it revealed again. John probable can continue to work with Red if he will remember to be quiet and to move slowly talking all the time maybe just telling Red what he is doing. Joe it will take you longer but the same methods can be helpful."

Fred announced that the steaks, sometimes called hamburgers, were ready to be flavored with mustard, ketchup, mayonnaise, lettuce, pickles, A-1 sauce and anything else in the kitchen. A second invitation was not needed. A delicious meal was topped off with chocolate cake and ice cream.

John and I excused ourselves for John to show me more

of the ranch headquarters. It's possible we also talked about A. & M. I found my mind again wondering in thoughts of this eventually being my home. They were fleeting thoughts, but I could not ignore them.

It had been a full but exciting day and the Johnsons were ready to enjoy the "modern" guest cabin. Carolyn said breakfast would be ready at seven and available until everyone had their fill of eggs, bacon, and sausage, home made rolls with jelly, jam and butter. John was going to participate in one of the calf roping events at the rodeo so everyone went to cheer for him. He won his event and I rewarded him with a red rose. The remainder of the visit included a tour of the ranch on horseback. Red walked up to me looking for a treat. I didn't have one but John did so Red went over to him and let John mount up.

"That's good, John because you will be here, and he will become your horse. If Star was here I was insist that she take me."

Like all good things, the visit came to a conclusion. We expressed our appreciation for the hospitality, and for the use of the guest cabin. John gave me a hug which I returned. George and Rosalyn found mutual interests and promised to stay in touch.

Graduation from high school was nice and parties were part of it. Now, it's on to Texas A. & M. The Goodnights and our family had another good visit as they settled their offspring into housing at college. They would miss them, but they were already sensing that they would be seeing more of each other. No one had put thoughts into words, but John and I were not missing any opportunity to be together. Both families approved.

College! This isn't high school! No one to wake us mornings or check our clothing. We are on our own, but we like it!

John and I took our meals in the school cafeteria, and made it a point to meet for the evening meal and some times at noon. After dinner the first day, we found a bench where we could sit and visit.

I liked my professors and I met several girls in my dorm that were friendly and one is majoring in psychology.

"Would you believe, my English professor wants us to write a theme each week? I thought I was through with English when I graduated from high school," was John's comment.

"What I like best about college is that I get to see you every day."

"It is nice, John. And Wednesday we get to play together in the orchestra."

Meeting for the first orchestra practice was fun. Dr. Foster asked each student to introduce themselves, tell what instrument they played and their hometown.

"Did any one have a camp last summer?"

"Jayda and I were at Interlockin for four weeks," mentioned John. "In fact, that is where we met. One of our fun projects was composing a duet for our clarinets."

"That is an outstanding camp. Your duet will be on our program when you are ready. Now let's make some music. In the key of C. Now a step up. Very good."

"Next session I will have some music on your racks and we will start on our fall program. John and Jayda, before you go if you have a few minutes I would like to hear a sample of your duet."

"How's your memory, John?"

"If you will start, I think I can follow."

"You are good, aren't you? Can you stretch it to two minutes?"

"No problem. We probably can add some orchestration to it."

"I am delighted to have you in our orchestra. Are you sure you don't want to major in music?"

"We enjoy music, but we have both set our sights on another major. We were excited when we learned we could keep our fingers in our clarinets during college."

The orchestra did provide John and me with a pleasant "extra" to our more serious classes in our major areas of study. I was able to put some orchestration to our duet, and it was added to the orchestra's library and proper copywriting filing was made in mine and John's names.

Daily communicating with each other moved John and I closer rather than bored ,and less interested in seeing each other. Between our sophomore and junior years we were spending Christmas at my home. Walking into the den under a wreath of mistletoe, John took me his arms and kissed me. To his joy I returned the kiss like a lady in love. Walking to the empty davenport, we sat down still holding on to each other. Taking my hands, John looked strait into my eyes and confessed,

"Jayda I love you. Will you marry me and be my partner as long as we live?"

"Yes, John I want to marry you and spend our lives together."

This called for another long and satisfying kiss. Just then

George walked into the room, and observing the situation asked, "When is the wedding?"

"As soon as possible. You want to be my best man?," replied John.

"Hey, Mom and Dad come in here and help plan a wedding."

Mother and Dad came into the room and sensing the situation reached out to embrace two happy sweethearts.

"I think it is customary for the man to ask parents permission to marry their daughter. Is it o.k.?"

"We have looked forward to this time for several months. You have our warm and sincere blessings. Help – and I emphasize the word help, plan your wedding. It will be your wedding, and we want it to be your way."

"I want to call my parents and Rosalyn. "

"Mother! I just asked Jayda to marry me and she said 'yes! I'm walking on cloud nine! No, we haven't talked about when. But we will. All of you must be apart of the wedding. Dad, you just got another daughter. Jayda agreed to be my bride for life."

"O.K. Jayda let's be halfway serious for a few minutes. When will you finish law school?"

"A year from next June. Then I will be ready to study for the bar exam."

"Mother, how long did Dad wait for you to finish law school?"

"Four years and three days!" answered Dad. "But it was worthy it. We began our marriage with nothing demanding our time except each other and it was wonderful."

"John and I need to go for a walk and talk. You may be sure we will be back for dinner."

After they walked out Frank told Jayme,

"Fred talked with me about his plans for John. Basically, he wants John to return to the ranch and gradually assume full control. He said he and Jayda (he had already assumed they would marry) can build somewhere on the ranch or he and Caroline might move and give them the ranch house. It will be a comfortable situation for all."

"We have decided to finish college before we get married,"announced Jayda as she and John returned from their walk. "When we get married we don't want anything in our way. It's going to be full steam ahead for the almost perfect marriage like both of our parents have. They are perfect role models for a satisfying marriage."

True to the experience of others, the last few months in college did not allow a lot of time for planning a marriage. John and I spent most of our free time telling each other how much we loved each other. We did give serious thought about dates and members of the wedding party. June tenth was selected as the date. It would be in the afternoon at my home church. Pastor Williams would conduct the ceremony. I wanted both my mother and John's mother to be matron of honor. I finally asked my mother who was thrilled to have that honor.

Thinking ahead, John realized he and his Dad needed to have some serious conversations.

"I have always dreamed of returning to the ranch after college, but we have not talked about the details. We need to be sure we have a meeting of minds. Jayda you are a part of my life, and I want it be the happiest one in the world."

"It will John a long as we are together in our dreams. Let's find a time soon when we can all talk together about our dreams for the future. Have you and Rosalyn ever talked about her feelings for the ranch? She has a vested interest in its future."

"No, I haven't. Let's talk with her first. Rosalyn! Can you spare a few minutes to talk business?"

"If it's not too serious, I'm available. Shall we meet on the porch?"

"Before we start I have a very important question, Rosalyn, will you be my brides maid in our wedding."

"Oh, yes, I want to be right in the middle of that event. Thank you for including me."

"Now John has a question."

"Do you have a dream about what you want to do or be in the next twenty or thirty years? Is there something that just comes to the surface when you think of the future?"

"I'm way ahead of you. Yes, I do dream of who I want to become. And it doesn't have anything to do with the ranch. That's your 'baby'. I dream of being a great trumpet player and playing in a large symphony orchestra. Along the way, another lover of music, handsome, gentle, fun and romantic will join my dream."

"That's my sister!" exclaimed John "She'll fulfill that dream and it wouldn't surprise me if she already has that 'other lover of music' in her sights. Thank you for sharing your dream with us."

"O. K. now tell me your dreams."

"Fair enough. We dream of being together for the rest of our lives. My dream has always been to return to the ranch after college, and join Dad in the business. He and I have not discussed this, but I think he will be agreeable. I want to be more involved in the business side, and somewhat less in rounding up of cattle and branding calves."

"Rosalyn, you have heard of my limited, but exciting role

helping children find their way in this world using my filly, Star. With my degree in psychology, I dream of continuing that role using the facilities of the ranch. I love the ranch and with John assuming more responsibility I cannot think of a better place to pursue the dream that first came to my mother."

"One more thing Rosalyn. We want you to know. However Dad and Mother decide to pass on their assets, Jayda and I will be sure you are an equal heir."

"Thanks, you beautiful and practical bride and groom. It is helpful to talk about ideas now when we are not under pressure to make decisions."

"We plan to ask all of our families to meet and have a similar discussion, but we wanted to talk with you first as your dreams are important in our planning. If you had said your dream was of coming back to the ranch, we would welcome you and that other lover of music, to a position of importance and pride at the ranch."

We did arrange for a meeting of our families and over cake and ice cream dreams were told and ideas exchanged. Dad admitted that he had looked forward to having John back at the ranch and now with Jayda joining the family his dream is being fulfilled.

Housing was discussed and at one point John's mother mentioned that she and Fred had talked about looking into the extended living home in San Angelo. That would leave the ranch house for John and Jayda.

"Mother, let me express a very strong opinion in favor of you and Dad staying in this house as long as either of you can draw a breath. Many studies have shown and people who work with mature adults, confirm the idea that moving from familiar and loved surroundings that you know by heart because you built them, will shorten your lives as much as twenty years. The finest facilities you can find do not change the results materially. For what you would pay a nursing home, you can hire trained help including registered nurses if needed."

"John, Rosalyn and I want to visit you often, but it will be more fun to visit you in the house that reminds us of you and the wonderful times we have had with you."

"I can confirm that fact from my law practice," added Jayme. "Fight to stay here until they call the funeral home."

"John and I can build a house on the ranch or elsewhere. Between us we can handle a mortgage."

Fred and Caroline thanked John,

Jayda and Rosalyn for sharing dreams and ideas with them. It was revealing but also reassuring. The meeting ended with a prayer of thanks for the family, and asking for continued guidance as life moved on. During the next few weeks John and his Dad worked out a written plan for John to move into the business of the ranch. His dad insisted that John and Jayda chose a hundred acres on the ranch for a homestead. John and I had already started drawing plans for the house we would build.

"Wedding plans were put on the 'front burner.' John and I finished classwork, and prepared for graduation. Preparation for the wedding became number one on our agenda. John and I were not much help with the details. We were occupied with the joy of being together every day all day. Our parents with the help of Rosalyn and George finally had the essentials in place."

"During the rehearsal dinner, Fred and Caroline had an opportunity to thank Jayda and Jayme for their recommendation that they (the Goodnights) plan to stay in their house rather than go to an assisted living facility. What a relief not to be thinking about moving. We didn't realize how much the idea of moving was disturbing us. We are so relaxed now knowing we can stay in 'our home.' Thank you."

"The wedding was all that a wedding of two wonderful, loving people should be. The church was tastefully decorated and everyone played their part. The Potters (remember Roger?) hosted a reception following the ceremony. Dad led the group in prayer thanking the Lord for Jayda and John, and asking for guidance as they embark on a life together. George was ready to drive the newlyweds on their honeymoon. Only the families knew they would stay in the guest cabin tonight, and leave in the morning for Hawaii on a ten day honeymoon."

Returning to the ranch, refreshed and ready to move on, we talked with Mother and Dad about the location of our new house. Dad's suggestion was in a grove of large oak trees with a broad view of the ranch. A small spring fed stream flowed along one side of area. There was a well nearby. I fell in love with it immediately and John said, "This is it!"

Now to fit the plans for the house on the site disturbing as few of the trees as possible. With some professional advice and Dad and John's knowledge of building, the new house was livable in three months and completed in six months."

****

Now it is time to say goodbye to Jayme and her family and thank them for many exciting events. Be assured there will be many more to come as Jayda and John build their family and move into their chosen roles in life.